I0600646

Water & Power

by Richard Montoya

A SAMUEL FRENCH ACTING EDITION

FOUNDED 1830

NEW YORK HOLLYWOOD LONDON TORONTO

SAMUELFRENCH.COM

ISBN 978-0-573-69647-3   Printed in U.S.A.   #29060

MUSIC USE NOTE

IMPORTANT BILLING AND CREDIT
REQUIREMENTS

The 2006 Ted Schmitt Award for the world premiere of an outstanding new play was awarded by the Los Angeles Drama Critics Circle to Richard Montoya for Culture Clash for *WATER & POWER*.

WATER & POWER premiered on July 27, 2006 at the Center Theatre Group's Mark Taper Forum in Los Angeles, California; Michael Ritchie, Artistic Director; Charles Dillingham, Managing Director; Gordon Davidson, Founding Artistic Director. The production was directed by Lisa Peterson with the following cast and creative team:

NORTE/SUR . . . . Ric Salinas

WATER (GILBERT GARCIA) . . . . Richard Montoya

POWER (GABRIEL GARCIA) . . . . Herbert Siguenza

ASUNCIÓN GARCIA . . . . Winston J. Rocha

DEER DANCER, GIBBY, GABBY . . . . Moises Arias

MINISTRO, VENDOR . . . . Emilio Rivera

THE FIXER . . . . Dakin Matthews

Set Design: Rachel Hauck
Costume Design: Christopher Acebo
Lighting Design: Alexander V. Nichols
Music And Sound Design: Paul James Prendergast
Dramaturg: John Glore
Fight Director: Steve Rankin
Choreographer: Jennifer Sanchez
Casting: Erika Sellin, CSA
Associate Producer: Kelley Kirkpatrick
Production Stage Manager: James T. Mcdermott
Stage Manager: Susie Walsh
Stagehands: IATSE Local 33

CHARACTERS

NORTE/SUR
WATER (GILBERT GARCIA)
POWER (GABRIEL GARCIA)
ASUNCIÓN GARCIA
DEER DANCER, GIBBY, GABBY
MINISTRO, VENDOR
THE FIXER

TIME

Before

PLACE

L.A.

El augua que no has de beber,
Dejala a corer.

The Water that you will not drink,
Let it run.

–Mexican saying

Danger: High Voltage Power lines underground.

–The DWP

There is a street in East LA, a street that separates the City from the County, The Cops from the Sheriffs. Garfield High from Roosevelt High,
And there were two little boys who danced beautifully between those two worlds, under the watchful eye of a father, where a Mother needed to be in theit fateful hour...

Water and Power.

(No pre-show music.)

(House slowly lights down.)

(A single drop of water becomes thunder & rain.)

(A rock song, something like Led Zeppelin's "The Rain Song" is heard.*)

(A shaft of bright light to cut a sharp contrast across the stage.)

(A figure comes through the door.)

(It is **NORTE/SUR**. *Wheelchair bound,* **NORTE/SUR** *is a Homeboy, a Vato from the street, a Veterano. He slowly wheels himself center stage then makes a large, ceremonial circle with his chair. He is deliberate, methodical, he rushes for nobody or anything.)*

(In a door or pathway The **DEER DANCER** *is revealed standing upstage right or left in the shaft of light.)*

(He is a boy, shirtless, in white peasant pants, shakers around his ankles, he holds a shaker and wears antlers atop his head. He does not move except for an occasional flick of the wrist, this allows us to hear his shakers.)

*See Music Use Note on page three

*(**NORTE/SUR** stops slightly up-center position, facing out. He reaches into the side bag of his chair, removing a black Piece Book – an art and poetry sketch book favored by graffiti artists – he opens the Piece Book – then slowly and respectfully closes it. He speaks to the audience.)*

NORTE/SUR. It's been raining for seventeen days and nights in LA.

Raining real hard. Could be that the Gods are pissed off about something. Yup, the Lords of Death are back in town. For sure. You have to be extra *trucha* with the Lords of Death, for they will cut you up just to see what you're made of inside, and you will thank them because they are charming. They can hide behind a badge or sit in the back seat with a shotgun. They wear pinstripes and broken promises. They can make trains jump the track, they know when its supper time at your *jefitas* house. The Lords of Death can look at you from the other side of the mirror and you would never know.

The Lords of Death like to punish us when we reach too high. What goes up must come down. Day/night. Good/evil. Life and death.

Smile now, cry later. 18 with a bullet. North. South. *Norte/Sur.*

Water and Power, torn together in that space between the Thunder and the Lightning where so much can happen, or nothing at all. Somebody prays for rain, somebody prays for it to stop. Record rainfall could wash LA away. I think the Lords of Death are fucking with us right now.

They like to throw us in the Dark House.

*(Thunder and **DEER DANCER** darts off.)*

Oddly enough, I'm looking for a Dark House right now. A place called the Motel Paradise, yup, you know it, you've driven passed it a hundred times, its one of those single story, sad affairs that snake up and down the eastside of anywhere, the eastern edge of Sunset Boulevard.

That's the part of the *boulee* that you never wanna find yourself, on a dark and rainy night.

(Big thunder, or a shotgun blast. They sound the same on nights like this.)

(Another rock song, something powerful like Led Zeppelin's "When the Levee Breaks"* slams in like a hammer.)

*(**NORTE/SUR** quickly pulls his hoodie over his head and dashes off.)*

(huge thunder)

*See Music Use Note on page three

Scene One

(Motel Paradise is revealed: a sad room complete with twin Patrick Nigel prints bolted to the wall, they have stood witness to years of unprotected sex.)

(One man forces his way into the room. There is an altercation.)

(fight)

(Two men struggle, there are weapons as one man forces the other on a bed. Freeze. The men are face to face. One man points his LAPD revolver to the other.)

WATER. Hi.

(beat)

(They embrace, then a powerful push away. These are the Brothers Gilbert and Gabriel Garcia, also know as **WATER** *and* **POWER.***)*

POWER. You – need – to – get – the – fuck – out- of – here, NOW!

WATER. Why are you hiding in this shit hole?

POWER. Don't ask.

*(***WATER*** sees a AK47 and a Mack 10 on bed and dresser.)*

WATER. Oh Jesus, shit, why do you have so many God-damned guns?

POWER. Who made you Mr. Consent Decree?

WATER. Have you been drinking again?

POWER. Get the fuck out of here senator. The shit is about to hit the fan.

WATER. What sort of trouble are you in?

POWER. Big.

WATER. How big?

POWER. There's been a breakdown.

WATER. What kind of breakdown?

POWER. Just a breakdown. That's all I can tell you.

WATER. Call for back up.

POWER. I *am* back up.

WATER. Great.

POWER. How did you know I was here?

WATER. You called me asshole.

POWER. The fuck I did.

WATER. I have a text message right here, Motel Paradise, see Power, room 13.

POWER. It wasn't me. I don't text.

*(**POWER** slams a magazine into his AK47 for punctuation.)*

POWER. It's gay.

WATER. Stop fucking around. I'm here already. What's up?

POWER. I'm in deep water.

WATER. How deep?

POWER. Over my head deep.

WATER. Yeah?

POWER. It's bad.

*(A Blackberry phone rings. **POWER** draws his gun. **WATER** <u>carefully</u> points to his coat pocket as an explanation:)*

WATER. My Blackberry. Easy.

(He looks at the call.)

WATER. I gotta get this. Sober up, fucko.

*(**WATER** answers.)*

WATER. Mister Speaker! Hey, no, perfect timing sir. Couldn't be better. What do you mean what's in the Green Bill? Have you read my fucking Green Bill?

*(**POWER** is lining up blow on the dresser.)*

WATER. It doesn't "pole well"? Were you not a radical hunger striker at Berkeley pal? Let me tell you something, from one humble public servant to another, this piece of fine legislation has real support, it's got coalition building all over it. I've got the teachers, the nurses, the Gay Latino Firefighters in fact I'm talking to the Police Union right now.

*(**POWER** does a blast of cocaine sounding like a small steam engine.)*

WATER. We're at Starbucks, more steam please.

C'mon BOB, co sign this thing with me, the leadership always follows you and I swear to God we'll have green space – a million fucking trees – on 40 acres of LA River on the Eastside. The Cesar Chavez River Walk Way.

As unlikely as a Cornfield in Chinatown.

How about less asthma for eastside third graders, huh? Why should kids west of the 405 get to breathe better air? Because you owe me fucker! Gotta go Bob. Late.

(**WATER** *hangs up as* **POWER** *does another huge blast of the blow.*)

WATER. What the hell are you doing you Hoover vacuum cleaner fuck?

POWER. Want a bump?

(**POWER** *is back at the yayo pile.*)

POWER. C'mon, do a bump with your bro.

WATER. I can't do blow with you.

POWER. Since when?

WATER. I'm running an important campaign at the moment fuck-stick.

POWER. You still boning your campaign manager?

(**WATER** *finds meds and an asthma inhaler on a bedside nightstand.*)

WATER. *(reading label)* Oxicontin.

(**WATER** *puts the bottle in his jacket. He picks up an asthma inhaler.*)

WATER. Sweet. Your inhaler is empty.

(**WATER** *picks up a triple beam scale used to measure drugs and precious gems. He reads a sticker on the scale:*)

WATER. Oh Jesus, "Do not remove from Rampart Evidence Room."

(*He discards it like a hot potato and wipes his prints off it.*)

POWER. It's okay, as long as you bring it back. It's like Net-flicks down there.

(**WATER** *picks up a big black binder.*)

WATER. LAPD Murder Book?

(**WATER** *looks through the book.*)

WATER. Who are all the dead guys?

(**POWER** *does a short blast.*)

POWER. Monsters. I chase monsters, bro. And if I have become a monster, then maybe that makes me a better monster catcher.

(**WATER** *tosses the book back on the bed.*)

POWER. You guys said "more cops on the street," that's what it looks like.

WATER. That was a campaign speech, asshole.

POWER. That's the problem with you guys, you don't mean what you say.

WATER. I stand by every word.

POWER. Did you not say "get drugs off the street?"

WATER. Absolutely.

(**POWER** *smiles and does another blast.*)

POWER. Well, I'm just doing my part, bro.

(**WATER** *lunges for the top of the dresser shoving the coke to the floor.*)

POWER. Hey! What the hell. Oh man. That was the last of my shit.

WATER. Good.

(**POWER** *picks up his stuff.*)

POWER. I haven't seen you in months, and now you come crashing my party? Fuck that, Gilbert.

WATER. I was gonna call, Gabe. Everything's been non stop, 24/7.

POWER. Everything is everything. Everything is everything.

POWER. I saw my daughter today.

WATER. Yeah?

POWER. God, her mom's a cunt. There's this picture of them on the fire place that *I* built. The new guy standing right there, holding my daughter man, like she was his. A few years ago that was me, you know. I was photo shopped right out of the fucking picture. Invisible. And the day started with so much promise.

WATER. *(relieved)* Is that what this is all about bro?

(**WATER** *places a brotherly hand on* **POWER***'s shoulder. Blackberry chirp.*)

POWER. Gonna answer your *crackberry?*

(Blackberry rings.)

WATER. Fu'uck. *(He answers.)* Bob? What do you mean you've got to ask Gloria first? Molina? No, LA County's fine with this. She'll be unhappy with me? She's from Pico Rivera, have you ever met a happy person from Pico fucking Rivera?

(**POWER** *is rifling through an old tool chest that reads D.W.P. on it.*)

WATER. East LA Machine politics babe, it still works. Old Man Roybal built it I just gotta live *in* it. Yes that is true, I'm getting very close to governor so I can't let this thing get derailed by the slightest or it's dead in the arroyo, I'll be floating face up in the Fernando Valenzuela Wash with my Tongva ancestors.

Do this for me and I'll get you T time at Pebble Beach for the Crippled

Chicano Children golf tourney! You can be the Great White Hope, all hero and shit.

Hey, hey, no need for name calling Bob, listen, I've been a Chicano since 1993, (**POWER** *re-enters from the john wearing sunglasses and LAPD jacket)*

What do you say pal? Uh, huh. Yes. Oh thank you assembly member. You are a rock star. Bless you for your support, sir. Green Space, it's so important man. One Million Trees in East LA! Thank you my Jewish brother. You just did one hell of a Mitzvah pal. Thank you dude! Mazeltov!

*(**WATER** hangs up his cell phone.)*

Oh yeah. That's how laws are made. Your brother is a stud, a proud progressive but still a stud.

*(**POWER** slams down his nightstick down on the dresser.)*

WATER. Whoa!

POWER. Fuckers lose respect for the badge, gotta go about things in a different fashion know what I mean bro?

WATER. What?

POWER. People see a cop...sometimes they isolate you. You find yourself all alone, out there, sometimes you got no choice but to bust a few bald *cholo* heads.

*(**POWER** slams the nightstick again.)*

WATER. Was that the "to protect" or "to serve" part of your job? Jesus.

(Another swift move with the baton and we know its deadly force.)

POWER. I wanted to be a cop for all of Los Angeles, but they wouldn't let me bro.

WATER. Who wouldn't let you?

POWER. Everybody on the other side of that door.

*(**POWER** does a long shot at Cuervo from the handle bottle.)*

WATER. This shit is making you paranoid and toxic.

POWER. Me toxic?

WATER. Uh, huh.

POWER. You would know. Weren't toxic land deals with minority developers your main boogie before you got on the green gravy train?

WATER. Fuck you softly...

POWER. Just making *abondigas* man, don't be such a pussy.

*(**POWER** places a hand on **WATER**'s shoulder, it almost comforts **WATER**.)*

POWER. Relax homey.

*(**POWER** runs his hand down the back of his brother's shoulder tenderly.)*

POWER. You wearing a wire? Huh? You wearing a wire little fucker?

(**POWER** *was serious.* **WATER** *squirms away.*)

POWER. *(cracking himself up)* Always wanted to say that. "You wearing a wire?"

WATER. Let's get the hell out of this shit hole right now, grab a cup of coffee. Sober up. Just you and me, like we used to.

POWER. Can't do.

WATER. Can do. I know a coupl'a detectives, Robbery Homicide guys, I'll make the call right now.

POWER. RHD? Hell no. You make that call my SWAT brothers are here inside three minutes, Tactical in four, Mental Assessment Response Team in five. Forensics before the sun comes up. They'll come like a hard rain for their own.

(**WATER**'s *Blackerry chirps: duty calls.*)

WATER. Speak. Dude, I can't get away. Cover my ass on the "Green Space Bill" for one hour, be my laser. Buy me some time, you are my bulldog assistant, do it, possess the skill set I taught you or I will send you back to you back to Id-a-fucking-ho where you came from. Go.

(**WATER** *hangs up and sees that* **POWER** *has slumped into an emotional state and clutches his chest.*)

WATER. Hey, hey now, what's going on over here...

POWER. My heart. Feel.

(**POWER** *places* **WATER**'s *hand on his heart.*)

WATER. Racing.

POWER. I know, huh.

(**WATER** *is taken aback for a moment when he sees something:*)

WATER. You got some blood on your badge bro, let me hit that for you.

POWER. Shaving. Must have cut myself a little too close to the bone.

(WATER cleans the blood with his kerchief.)

WATER. Yeah. Good to go.

POWER. Good to go. Who ah!

(POWER playfully punches WATER in the gut. WATER tries to calm him.)

WATER. Easy now. Gabe sit down. Hey, do you remember, remember that time Dad told us to beat the crap outta each other?

POWER. When did he say that?

WATER. That time he made us box in front of his *compadres.*

POWER. Oh *yeah that* time. That was brutal man.

WATER. Nah, we got a little bloodied that's all.

POWER. I got bloodied Bro.

(POWER sits across from the bed on a hotel chair.)

WATER. I was bigger than you then Gabe.

POWER. Once upon a time.

WATER. On those Eastside streets babe.

POWER. I could always dance though, bro. Dad learned me to bob and weave real good. That was the difference. Then I could go toe to toe with you.

WATER. You did beat the shit out of me that time we fought in the Secret Circle.

(We hear children playing in the distance.)

(A slow smile crosses POWER's face. WATER coaxes POWER's grin.)

WATER. You remember that bro? It's a fond memory for you isn't it. Let me see that smile. What's up *carnal*? What sort of trouble are you in lieutenant?

(WATER places a tender kiss on his brother's cleanly shaven head.)

WATER. There you go, Gilbert and Gabriel. Gibby and Gabby. The Twins. Together again. Remember those guys, bro?

POWER. Water & Power baby.

WATER. Estrada Courts to the max.

POWER. Barrio Nuevo.

WATER. Where ever we went.

POWER. Who *ever* we met.

WATER. The Russian's on Lorena Street. Bologna sandwiches from *Angel's* Market. *Spam* when we were *good*.

POWER. We're a long way from Costello Park, bro.

WATER. Dacotah Street is just down the road.

POWER. Seems far, like way down there.

(pointing off then a deep breath)

POWER. Woosh. Weird.

WATER. Easy.

(A sudden energy surge from **POWER** *as he rises from his chair.)*

POWER. Montebello Nights!

WATER. With our Beatle Boots? You thought you were a Jetter man.

POWER. *Chale* homes, I was a Phantom.

WATER. I thought you were in the Magic Club?

POWER. No, from the heart of the ghetto and shit homeboy.

(That gets a chuckle from **WATER.** *)*

POWER. Water and Power strutting to the Friday night football games. Shit, even the brothers from 103rd Street respected us.

WATER. That's because we *respected* the brothers from Watts.

POWER. I heard that niggah!

WATER. N. Shhh…

POWER. Little Hazzard, Happy Valley, *Maravilla*, we went everywhere, homes.

*(***WATER** *sits back in the chair and shines his shoes.)*

WATER. Actually, we never went to *Maravilla*, it was too dangerous.

(We hear distant popping. **POWER** *crouches like a soldier.)*

POWER. *(whisper)* Hear that bro?

WATER. What?

POWER. Firing range at the academy, right on time.

WATER. Maybe it's some *cholo's* down the street.

POWER. No. Above the lodge, Elysian Park.

WATER. How can you be certain.

POWER. Short blasts. Rata tat tat shit. Impatient cop action. Strictly 9 millimeter.

*(**POWER** climbs on a hotel chair, draws his weapon and strikes his expert firing pose.)*

WATER. Easy. Easy.

(We hear a distant train whistle.)

POWER. Union Station, right on time too.

*(**POWER** checks his watch. We hear Ranchero music from a distant nightclub.)*

WATER. You had to pick the loneliest mile on Sunset boulevard.

POWER. It ain't so bad.

WATER. The Life of Riley over here.

*(Far upstage of the action, a **MAN** slowly across the stage, with large water bottles)*

POWER. Listen!

*(We hear far off **CHOIR VOICES**:)*

CHOIR VOICES. …augua que va El Senor Jesus Cristo…

POWER. The Mexican Evangelical storefronts.

*(**WATER** hears this.)*

POWER. Damn, the city is working tonight.

WATER. Just like Dad used to say bro.

(From offstage we hear the stern yet loving voice of:)

FATHER. *(offstage)* Boys! C'mon.

(Dad's familiar whistle.)

WATER. Breath brother. Breathe.

*(**POWER** takes a deep breath and doubles over.)*

WATER. Good.

FATHER. *(offstage)* Let's go boys.

> (**POWER** *crumples as* **WATER** *helps him down from the chair.*)

WATER. You gotta calm down lieutenant, pull it up. You've got to tell me what went down tonight bro, walk me through it, all of it.

POWER. I'm hanging on here, bro.

WATER. I'll hang with.

POWER. I may need a good lawyer.

WATER. You know I'm a lawyer, *cabron.*

POWER. I said a *good* lawyer.

> (**WATER** *starts to clear the bed of weapons.*)

POWER. My brother, graduated from the Peoples Law School! 300th in your class. Passed the bar on his 13th try. Perry Mason in the house.
> I got in an accident and my brother got me 500 dollars!

WATER. Okay.

POWER. Shit, all your Latino elected's have their law degrees, but they're *escared* to take the bar. That's chicken shit, but not my bro. You got balls Gibby.

WATER. You gonna tell me what happened to you?

POWER. Can you *handle* it bro?

WATER. Got to.

POWER. Because you were always kind of a pussy about shit like this.

WATER. I'm with you now Gabe. And what ever it is we'll flip it. We have the skill set. What would pop say? Pop would say that every situation has pluses and minuses, together we'll find the pluses.

POWER. Water and Power?

WATER. That's right. Dad's Pride and Joy.

POWER. Those brothers were blessed.

WATER. We're still blessed bro.

POWER. You think?

WATER. Oh yeah.

POWER. You gonna back my play, Gibby?

WATER. What ever it is, we'll handle it. Okay?

(**WATER** *flashes his confident smile for good measure.*)

POWER. Don't leave me here, bro.

WATER. I couldn't do that.

POWER. *(awe)* LA is full of ghosts man.

(*We hear thunder.*)

WATER. Don't go there man.

POWER. Okay. Right.

WATER. Right.

(**WATER** *has made it better and smiles at his bro.*)

POWER. I killed a man tonight.

(**WATER**'*s smile goes away.*)

POWER. Killed him. Sure enough.

(*Enter a young* **GILBERT GARCIA/WATER** *and his father* **ASUNCION GARCIA.***)

(**MR. GARCIA** *wears D.W.P. work overalls with his name tag and department logo of that era. He places a chair just downstage of the previous Motel scene.* **WATER & POWER** *never leave the stage.*)

Scene Two

*(Enter **ASUNCION GARCIA**: Department of Water and Power reservoir and irrigation field man in Southern California wears thick black glasses of that era. Father is followed by a young **GILBERT GARCIA/WATER**.)*

*(**MR. GARCIA** wears D.W.P. work overalls with his name tag and department logo of that era.)*

*(**LITTLE GIBBY** has on boxing headgear and converse lace up sneakers. Father holds up his dukes as "Gibby" punches them like a little tough guy and quite a good little fighter.)*

FATHER. Did you knock the shit out of your brother like I told you mijo?

(The boy shrugs.)

FATHER. Where is he?

GIBBY. In the room crying like a little pussy.

FATHER. *Por que mijo?* Why is he crying?

GIBBY. Because I hit him.

FATHER. With a hook or an uppercut?

GIBBY. With a flurry of jabs!

FATHER. Atta boy.

*(**GIBBY** strikes a Pachuco pose.)*

GIBBY. Just call me Golden Gloves ese!

*(**FATHER** smacks him upside the head.)*

GIBBY. Ouch.

FATHER. Don't get cocky little man.

GIBBY. Yes sir.

FATHER. Did you shine your black shoes like I told you at least?

GIBBY. Not yet, pop.

FATHER. *Chingow. Como eres* Gilbert.

GIBBY. Wool... *(well)*

FATHER. Como que wull?

(yelling off)

FATHER. GABBY!

POWER. *(upstage of the scene)* I don't feel good dad!

FATHER. Chihuahua, your brother is going to be late for his own damn funeral.

GIBBY. *(sort of confused)* A funeral for Gabby?

FATHER. Gilbert, your brother, how do I say it, well, he's slower than you. He doesn't use his *cabeza.*

GIBBY. Is he a retard dad?

FATHER. Well, mijo, I'm gonna tell you something and I want you to listen extra good, okay?

GIBBY. Sure dad.

FATHER. Always, always no matters what, look after your brother, look after him real good. Never ever leave him alone somewhere's. Where you go he goes, always watch his back, me entiendez?

*(**GIBBY** nods yes.)*

FATHER. Now repeat what I just said, cabron.

GIBBY. Okay. Repeat what I just said, cabron.

(That garners a slap upside the head.)

GIBBY. Ouchie, why do I always have to do the work?

FATHER. Because you were born first, mijo.

GIBBY. I know, I know. 8 minutes and 59 seconds.

FATHER. And there was lightening mijo...

*(**GIBBY** makes lightening sounds.)*

FATHER. ...and there was Thunder...

*(**GIBBY** makes big thunder sounds.)*

FATHER. And my little vatos were born between the...

FATHER/GIBBY. ...the lightening and thunder!

GIBBY. Wait a minute. Dad?

FATHER. Si?

GIBBY. Am I supposed to look after Gabby or beat him up?

FATHER. Both.

GIBBY. At the same time?

FATHER. Shut up mijo. Lookie, here's the plan: You and I will secretly tuff'n him up. And before you know it, he'll clobber your cabeza like Archie Moore and you won't even know what hit you. Just like the Mongoose!

(**GIBBY** and **DAD** *"slow motion boxers" with the Mongoose punch.*)

And you will pick yourself up off that canvas and look at your brother in the eyes and you will have new respect for him! Vale la pena! And then my boys will be the Twin Mirrors of Eastside Toughness. And people will have to respect you or else.

GIBBY. Why do they have to respect us Dad? We're not rich, we're nobodies.

FATHER. Let me tell you something about respect, mijo. You know the little old white lady on the corner? The one that goes to shursh every day?

GIBBY. Church?

FATHER. Si, shursh. See, I know sometimes she doesn't have enough to eat but you know what? She carries herself a si, con mucho dignidad. Always dressed to he nines. Everything in its place. Self respect, mijo. She has it.. Respect yourself Gilbert. Always.

GIBBY. Okay Dad.

(*If* **DAD** *crouches down* **GIBBY** *should mimic him*)

FATHER. And one day, when you and your brother are all grown up, you can help that old lady.

GIBBY. How old is she?

FATHER. I don't know, como seventy five or so.

GIBBY. Well, when we're grown up, won't she be dead already?

FATHER. You think you're so smart Carbon.

GIBBY. You just said I was smart Dad.

FATHER. Pinche morro…

GIBBY. Ooh, you said a bad word Dad.

(**DAD** *mumbles to himself.* **GIBBY** *exits.*)

GIBBY. Oh brother, now I'm confused and full of rage.

Scene Three

*(Back at the Motel Paradise. **WATER** is seated at the end
of the bed with his head buried in his hands. **POWER**
stands, very still, smoking.)*

POWER. After I got off my shift, I "borrowed" an unmarked
cruiser from Parker Center Garage, I had put Dad's
old D.W.P. overalls in the trunk the day before, waved
at the City parking guy as I pulled out of the garage,
changed clothes under the 4th street bridge, I was
methodical bro, covered my tracks, I rolled back to the
neighborhood, close to where we used to live, must
have been about 7, quarter past. My Monster, Mr. Pelican Bay released from prison early this morning, goes
to his mom's house to have supper in East LA, I know
it will be like his first or second stop, I waited for him
across the street in the unmarked car, just a few houses
down from Dad's old house.

WATER. Oh Jesus...

*(**WATER** crosses down and sits at the chair.)*

POWER. Not much street traffic.

*(We see a **MEXICAN MAN/VENDOR** carrying a water
bottle on his shoulder as he crosses upstage or the shadows of the round.)*

VENDOR. *(distant) Agua...agua...agua...*

POWER. I wait. I luck out big time because the guy goes to
see his *jefita* alone. A few more minutes, let him get
settled in with Mom's, I'm in the house like in nothing
flat, this house, it's dark inside, just one light on like
the house where the *Tecatos* go to O.D.
TV is blasting, *novellas* and shit, Mexican radio from
next door covers me, I mean it's perfect bro. Beautiful, seems fake almost: the little dining room separated
from the kitchen, I luck out again, Mom is back and
forth with the tortillas and stuff, my guy hasn't seen a
"home cooked" in ten to fifteen. He greazes down like
a hungry animal. I'm hanging back in the shadows.

*(**POWER** nods. A long drag off the cig.)*

POWER. I wait for just the right moment, Mom's fussing over some wedding and *quinciniera* pictures in the back room, my guy gets off his cell phone, kicks off his black shoes, television, radio, perfect level, I tip toe right behind the guy, I can smell the three flowers in his hair, I'm like this close. He's got a small <u>four leaf clover</u> tattooed on the side of his neck, must be new, wasn't in his file jacket...

*(**POWER** moves in behind **WATER** at the chair. **POWER** is using **WATER** as a sort of prop as continues to explain the murder.)*

Food smelled good, bro. Real good. His cell phone rings, shit, he looks at the number, does not take the call. I catch another break.

*(**POWER** pulls out the weapon, a beautiful little killing machine, he does so with slow methodical arm movements.)*

Silencer.

(He places a lovely silencer on the end of the firearm.)

I ask forgiveness for what I am about to do.

*(**POWER** points the gun to the back of **WATER**'s head.)*

Everything stops, I can't hear the TV blasting anymore. My heart is pounding. Another shadow outside in the yard!

*(The **DEER DANCER** crosses and is gone like a vapor.)*

POWER. It passes. I gotta go now. Lift gun to back of head.

*(**POWER**'s arm slowly raises into position just behind **WATER**'s head.)*

POWER. *(softly)* Pow.

*(We hear an echo of a gun blast in the distance. **WATER** moves his head in a fashion of a murder victim in super slow motion.)*

POWER. *(softly)* Pow. Pow.

*(Another echo for each gun blast in the distance. **POWER** looks right.)*

POWER. I don't know how long his mother was standing there but she's watching from the kitchen door way.

WATER. *(quietly realizing)* God dammit, no...

POWER. Oh yes. She was probably there the whole damn time you know, at first I just shined her on, but she kept screaming for her baby. My Monster. She's screaming but nothing is coming out, or maybe I just can't hear her I dunno. She stares at me, Gilbert. Her son's brains splattered all over the JFK and Jesus velvet paintings. I lift my gun to her.

*(**POWER** points his gun out.)*

She looks at me, calm suddenly, not crying, not screaming, she makes the sign of the cross and then she does the same for me.

*(**POWER** slowly makes the sign of the cross with the gun the way the Senora must have done for him: arm stretched out.)*

Why would she do that Gibby? My gun just fell to my side, I backed out slowly, I left her there standing silent in her kitchen doorway.

She saw it Gilbert, she saw the whole thing. She looked deep into me, man, right through me. I've never seen that look before. She's gonna remember my face. She's gonna have me etched across her brain, like a laceration.

WATER. Oh, Gabby, Gabby, Gabby...

POWER. I dropped some stuff off at the Taylor Yards incinerator, threw dad's overalls, Monster's cell phone in the fire. And that's it.

WATER. That's it?

POWER. Well, no. I mean P.D. is gonnna be looking for me, *and La EME.*

WATER. Well, opposites do attract, Gabriel.

POWER. Tonight they do. And they're gonna come hard.

WATER. Tell me, *why* did you clip the guy?

POWER. <u>LA is not for everybody.</u>

WATER. What the hell does that mean?

POWER. I had my reasons.

WATER. What possible reasons could you have to murder a man who had already served his time?

POWER. I did what I had to do. That's all I can say.

WATER. Oh God, you've been advising Homeland Security on LA Prison gangs.

POWER. Affirmative.

WATER. Well you'll need to say a whole lot more, lieutenant.

POWER. Negative. That's a no-go. I'm not talking about this with you.

WATER. I'm calling the LAPD negotiator right now.

POWER. The negotiator I know is also a sharpshooter. So that's not an option.

WATER. That's brilliant, Gabriel.

POWER. I'm serious as a heart attack bro. I know too much. Other cops will want me out of the picture.

WATER. Goddamn it, I knew it. Something was coming.

POWER. What?

WATER. Something would hit me here, hard. I would take some sort of blow, in the solar plexus. You used to knock the wind out of me. Just like that. I felt it earlier today, I swear to God I did. I did not know what to expect when I showed up here, but not this, not what I see now.

POWER. Gee, sorry bro. Hey, I need to re-up. Where's my guy?

(**NORTE/SUR** *bursts through the door. Thunder. Lights flicker.* **POWER** *draws his weapon, a split second of silence then recognition.*)

NORTE/SUR. Ese Power, Pelican Bay is all over the house. Word got out quick ese.

POWER. Which house?

NORTE/SUR. Your house, your father's old house. There's a shot-caller convention on the Eastside, aye.

POWER. Anybody follow you here?

NORTE/SUR. Yeah, three paisas and a border brother but they're cool.

POWER. Don't fuck around. Who's at my house exactly?

NORTE/SUR. Real shooters, no spray and pray guys.

POWER. *(more amazed and excited than angry)* You hear that, bro?

NORTE/SUR. And there's two Monterey Park dudes at the 7-11 by the crib.

POWER. *Vatos* from Monterey Park?

NORTE/SUR. No. Chinos, Asian cats. Fast and Furious *vatos.* Good cutters, expert knife guys.

POWER. *(This is big.)* They're going multi-cultural on my ass, huh?

WATER. *(cynical)* Coalition building...

POWER. *(hope)* Like Obama.

NORTE/SUR. Haters front to back. La Eme galore, 10%'ers, they got it wired tight this time. And cops I ain't never seen before creepy crawling all over the ghetto. Bookoo *jura.* The barrio is going berserk tonight.

(**NORTE/SUR** *looks to* **WATER.**)

NORTE/SUR. What's up?

(**WATER** *nods.*)

POWER. What did Chunky say?

NORTE/SUR. Couldn't get a hold of him at first.

POWER. Did you try his Blackberry.

NORTE/SUR. *Chale,* all the homey's have switched to Trio's. Some sort of wireless promotion sweeping the hood. Luckily, Chunky still keeps an old school pager.

POWER. Fascinating! And?

NORTE/SUR. He say's no "get out of jail cards," "get out of morgue cards" maybe.

POWER. That's kinda funny. Was he trying to be funny?

NORTE/SUR. Laughed *my* ass off.

WATER. And you are?

NORTE/SUR. *Despensa* homes. Mister *Norte/Sur.*

WATER. Mister what?

NORTE/SUR. *Norte/Sur.* I'm the one who texted you.

WATER. How the fuck did you get my number?

NORTE/SUR. I googled you. I put in Facebook friend request but you haven't responded. I been on pins and needles for weeks.

POWER. Why the fuck did you contact my brother?

NORTE/SUR. I had my reasons. Yeah, I see your pictures in the paper all the time, you're skinny homes.

POWER. This is my guy, bro.

WATER. This is your back up?

POWER. Shake his hand.

> (**NORTE/SUR** *tries again with the shake.* **WATER** *does not offer his hand.*)

NORTE/SUR. I ain't trippen aye.

> (**NORTE/SUR** *notices something.*)

NORTE/SUR. Hey man, who put the hat on the bed? It's bad luck aye.

> (**NORTE/SUR** *flings the hat off the dresser.* **WATER** *retrieves it.*)

NORTE/SUR. Ese Power, this whole *chingadrea* is much more serious than I thought. Worser even than when that Latino CHP cop *vato* got wasted.

WATER. Oh God.

NORTE/SUR. The *vato* you off'd was no soldier Gabe, he was way up the food chain, you know.

POWER. Okay! This is what I need, first, go the last Picnic Table on the northwest corner of Elysian Park, under that table is a brown bag, get it.

NORTE/SUR. *Simon.*

POWER. Then release the pigeons on top of the roof at the Sir Palmer apartments.

NORTE/SUR. On Echo Park Avenue?

POWER. *Simon.* Then cross the street put the bag under the boardwalk next to paddle boat number six.

NORTE/SUR. Got it.

POWER. After that pick me up a Jamba Juice with a protein boost in it.

NORTE/SUR. *(repeating and taking note)* Protein boost...

POWER. Then go to the car wash they're throwing for the dead homey.

NORTE/SUR. They're having a car wash for Mono?

POWER. No, for the homey that *killed* Mono.

NORTE/SUR. I can't go to Tripper's car wash aye.

POWER. Go to Toker's car wash then.

NORTE/SUR. Okay. Wait, what am I doing at the car wash again? It's raining cats and dogs out there.

POWER. Tell *Chele* to clean the inside of my car extra good, I want it smelling nice when they come for me. Have him put in some air fresheners.

NORTE/SUR. Lemon lime or midnight cherry?

POWER. You chose.

NORTE/SUR. *Cholo's* choice. Done.

POWER. And find Fucker Joey.

NORTE/SUR. What on earth do you want with Fucker Joey?

POWER. Tell him I'm gonna need some Pico Rivera muscle.

NORTE/SUR. Oh shit.

POWER. *Kique* from Clover ain't going to be happy.

WATER. Pico Rivera Muscle?

POWER. You got a point bro, make that Atwater Village Muscle.

NORTE/SUR. Why not go with Frog Town Muscle?

POWER. Too close to Toonerville Muscle.

NORTE/SUR. They're out of commish que no?

POWER. No, they just dress nice now.

NORTE/SUR. Like the Vineland Boys.

POWER. Ask him to check on Diamond Bar muscle.

NORTE/SUR. Won't that cause a conflict vis-à-vis the proximity to Canoga Park muscle?

POWER. Fuck it, let them work it out.

NORTE/SUR. Cool. What about Los Feliz Muscle?

POWER. Never.

NORTE/SUR. Why not break a little taste off for the Ceder Block Piru Bloods?

WATER. Los Feliz Muscle?

NORTE/SUR. I'm gonna have to make a muscle spread sheet.

POWER. Fuck it. Go to the LA River. Under the 6th street bridge you can wheel yourself through the tunnel leading all the way to the river bottom, find the homeless guy sleeping under a silver space blanket there, he looks like a miniature Disney Hall, ask him if Black Butch is out of the joint yet.

(**NORTE/SUR** *writes down:*)

NORTE/SUR. Find the Miniature Frank Gerry.

POWER. Then find White Butch and get 13 Dodger tickets, lower loge only, then go to Home Depot on San Fernando Road and get me some plastic tarpaulin. Go.

(**NORTE/SUR** *begins to shove off.*)

POWER. Hold up. Call Casper from a landline, tell him, no, better yet ask him nicely as a favor, to give me a freeway shooting on the Harbor in a bout an hour. No body gets killed though.

(**NORTE/SUR** *takes careful note.*)

NORTE/SUR. Victimless freeway shooting for cover.

POWER. After that go to Venice.

NORTE/SUR. *Chale*, can't go there aye. I got beef with that Shore Line Crips set.

POWER. Get out to Malibu as quick as you can.

NORTE/SUR. Malibu? I'm on the bus homes!

POWER. No excuses tonight Norte/Sur! Call fucking Henry at the MTA and get an all night Metro Link Pass.

NORTE/SUR. I don't take trains homey.

POWER. Hit Temescal Canyon before they close the gate, at the top of the trail is a waterfall, say three Hail Mary's, one for each of us in the room here.

WATER. I don't want his prayers.

NORTE/SUR. Water not cooperating. This is gonna take some time aye, and handicapped service is limited on rainy days.

POWER. Okay, forget Malibu. Hit Topanga, tell the Nazi Lowriders I need my guns back tonight. Period.

NORTE/SUR. And things were going so well with the Aryan Brotherhood. Anything else?

(**NORTE/SUR** *takes a final careful note.*)

(*There is a noise outside.* **POWER** *pulls up a side arm.*)

POWER. What the fuck was that?

(**NORTE/SUR** *out the curtain. A* **BAREFOOTED GUY** *streaks by dropping something.*)

NORTE/SUR. Calm down *ese.* It's only the barefooted Guatemalans delivering the LA Times.

POWER. They still got delivery boys in LA?

NORTE/SUR. Yeah, even though circulation is down.

POWER. Stealth bastards. They look hungry, must be on some good yay-yo. You'll need to hump like them if <u>we</u> plan to see tomorrow.

(**NORTE/SUR** *throws* **POWER** *a tied up bundle.*)

POWER. What's this?

NORTE/SUR. *Mota* laced with a touch of X to help you cope till I get back.

POWER. Who's it from?

NORTE/SUR. My homeboy Puppet, with warm regards.

POWER. Which Puppet?

NORTE/SUR. My Puppet.

POWER. And what Puppet is that exactly?

NORTE/SUR. You know, *ese* Puppet *ese vato loco* homeboy Puppet.

POWER. I didn't know *you* had a Puppet Norte/Sur.

WATER. What does it matter which fucking Puppet it is?

POWER. Actually it does matter bro, I mean there is a lot of Puppets in LA man.

NORTE/SUR. Here we go again.

POWER. I mean there's Big Puppet, Little Puppet, Medium Puppet, Super sized Puppet, Puppet with curly fries, Economy Puppet, Puppet Master...

NORTE/SUR. Don't get all crazy, aye.

POWER. Well I know a lot of Puppets. So again I ask Norte/ Sur, which fucking Puppet?

NORTE/SUR. And for the last time I'm telling you, *my* Puppet.

POWER. Put something on it. Put something on it, homes. *Cholo* up dog.

NORTE/SUR. *Cholo* up? Fuck you, you know that.

POWER. Hustle it up so you can get back here and shave my head, *nigga*...

NORTE/SUR. Real good to see you here with your carnal *ese* Mister Water. I've heard nothing but wonderful things about you from your fucked up brother over there. Could I bother you for an autograph in my piece book?

POWER. Save it for the book fair.

(**POWER** *stand by the door.* **NORTE/SUR** *heads for the door, he looks to* **POWER.**)

NORTE/SUR. Almost forgot to tell you, three of the rooms here at the motel are occupied tonight.

POWER. How many?

(*one final read from his Piece Book*)

NORTE/SUR. Five souls in all.

POWER. Shit.

NORTE/SUR. Everybody waiting for something in LA to-night.

(*beat as* **NORTE/SUR** *takes in the room a final time*)

Water and Power in the same room, damn, this must be bad.

POWER. Go!

NORTE/SUR. Gone.

(**POWER** *shuts the door and* **NORTE/SUR** *is gone. Thunder.*)

WATER. What the fuck was that? Who is that guy?

POWER. Somebody I trust.

WATER. He shouldn't be here.

POWER. He's my biographer.

WATER. Your what?

POWER. He's a writer.

WATER. Bullshit, he's a banger and he brings you drugs.

POWER. He's the one thing I've done right LA. I love that *cholo* like a brother.

WATER. I am your brother, Gabe.

POWER. I love him like you then.

WATER. Fuck that.

> (**WATER** *grabs the "Puppet" dope and tosses it on the dresser.*)

POWER. At first I didn't like him, but after I shot him, I did.

WATER. You shot Mapquest?

POWER. Twice. *Vato's* got a lot of heart. I figured if he survived my bullets, then maybe I'm supposed to look after him. We've been through a lot. He's in my car.

WATER. What car?

POWER. He rides shotgun. You're either in my car or your not, you're not in my car, homes.

WATER. When did you start talking like this, lieutenant?

POWER. Don't trip. He's my guardian angel.

WATER. You're a regular Father Boyle.

POWER. Like I said I trust him.

WATER. I'll be in your fucked up car if that's what you want, Gabe.

POWER. I don't want you in my car.

> (**WATER** *whips out his Blackberry.*)

WATER. I gotta go talk to a guy.

POWER. What guy?

WATER. The only guy I know that can fix your mess.

POWER. I don't know your guy. I can handle it my way.

WATER. You're way don't work, bro.

POWER. It worked every time I saved *your* ass.

WATER. Why do you always have to be the "fuck up brother"?

POWER. At least I'm not the "sell out brother."

WATER. I have never sold out.

POWER. You believe your own bullshit?

WATER. I believe what dad expected of us. And, this is *not* what he wanted, Gabe.

POWER. I honestly don't remember what that was anymore.

WATER. He wanted us to be *those* men Gabe.

POWER. What men?

WATER. Those big guys, man. Standing tall in their fine black shoes. God dammit, Gabe. Straight shooters, bro. Walking the line. Spit shined Garcias. The pride of East Los *ese*, champions of the little guy.

Warriors groomed like *gallos* by Henry and the Old Man, handpicked from a crowded field by the Berman Brothers themselves, with full blessings from Richard *and* Gloria. The Machine. The people who helped you get into the Academy.

WATER. *(cont.)* Do you remember them lieutenant? Dad's Eastside supers stars who would never ever forget the people in the housing projects. Yet tonight the Garcia brothers do not hear you poor people. We do not protect you and we sure in the fuck do not serve you because the bro's are in this fucked up room of yours and the shiny black shoes our father broke his back to give us are soiled and scuffed. And we will be way off the mark now. Thanks once again to your major lack of judgment, lieutenant.

*(**WATER** heads for the door.)*

POWER. Gilbert?

WATER. *(patience has run out)* What?

POWER. Save your guy for a rainy day.

(distant thunder.)

WATER. It's that rainy day.

*(Lightning then thunder and **WATER** is gone.)*

Scene Four

(On another part of the stage **FATHER** *is shadow boxing like a veterano. Expertly bobbing and weaving.)*

*(***GABRIEL*** *enters. Little* **GABBY/POWER** *is shirtless with Converse sneakers, red Boxing Shorts and matching, huge red boxing gloves with protective head gear. Mexican radio is faintly in the air.)*

GABBY. Dad? Dad?

FATHER. Si mijo?

GABBY. I feel like shit Dad.

FATHER. Que paso slugger? Por que 'stas llorando?

GABBY. Gilbert says I'm a Mexican retard is it true, pop?

FATHER. Well mijo, let's just say that Gilbert got the brains but you got the bolas.

GABBY. But my weener is small, dad.

FATHER. It'll grow mijo.

GABBY. Like yours pop?

FATHER. Oh *si.* Mas grande probably.

GABBY. Nooooo!

(Good news for **GABBY.** **FATHER** *puts a kerchief to son's nose. He blows.)*

FATHER. Blow.

*(***GABBY*** *blows.)*

FATHER. Again *mijo.* Are you keeping up your dukes at least?

GABBY. Yeah but Gilbert swings real fast that fucker.

FATHER. *Oh!* With the language.

*(***GABBY*** *laughs a little delighted, devilish laugh.)*

FATHER. You little *cabrones* talk like midget truck drivers. What's wrong with you *gueyes?*

GABBY. What's a way?

FATHER. Never mind, look son, on the level, you have to protect yourself son, *mira* when your brother comes in with his quick jabs, surprise him with a left hook. And you know what? He'll never expect it. And I'll give you a silver dollar if you knock him on his *nalgas.*

*(***GABBY*** *likes the idea a lot and laughs.)*

FATHER. And then I'll take you up to the reservoir with me.

GABBY. I'll shine my shoes extra good!

FATHER. Excellent idea. *Mijo.*

GABBY. That would be the best day in the whole wide world.

FATHER. What does it say on my shirt right here?

(Reading and pointing with an index finger the way children do.)

GABBY. The Department of Water and Power, City of Los Angeles.

FATHER. *Es todo mijo.* See, your brother is my Water, and you are my Power. Vez?

GABBY. Maybe I should be Water dad?

FATHER. No, no *mijo*, you are my Power.

GABBY. But I don't wanna be Power, I wanna be Water!

FATHER. No mijo, Gibby is already *mi aguita*, and you are my *Poder.*

GABBY. But Gibby get's everything.

FATHER. Lookie here little *vato.*

GABBY. Can I be the Gas Company?

FATHER. No.

GABBY. Can I be the fire department then?

FATHER. Ya Gabby, ya...

GABBY. Maybe I don't wanna be a utility company.

*(**FATHER** sits **GABBY** down on his knee.)*

FATHER. You are Power and you should be really, really happy with that.

GABBY. Why?

FATHER. Because.

GABBY. Because why?

FATHER. *Porque* under the city right now, there are these big turbines, see...

GABBY. What's a turbine?

FATHER. Like a giant propeller.

GABBY. How big is it pop?

FATHER. Bigger than our house.

GABBY. Nooooo.

FATHER. Oh siiiiiii.

GABBY. Nooooo.

FATHER. Uh huh, and the rushing waters turn the giant turbines and that's how we make the power that runs the city. And if you listen carefully, you can hear those turbines spinning under the earth. They never stop *mijo*, always moving like an octopus, feeding the city because she never stops eating like a monster. Listen carefully, *mijo*.

*(**GABBY** takes an impatient beat, his head moving like an inquisitive puppy as **DAD** makes arm motions to help **GABBY** imagine.)*

GABBY. Can't hear a thing pop.

FATHER. Get on the floor there, put your ear on the ground just like an Indian. Go on son.

*(**GABBY** happily squirms on the floor.)*

FATHER. *Calmate.*

*(**GABBY** settles down.)*

FATHER. Listen real hard *mijo*. Listen real close.

GABBY. I CAN'T HEAR A THING!!!

*(**FATHER** goes down on one knee to calm **GABBY** and get him to listen more carefully.)*

FATHER. Shhh.

GABBY. Wait a sec, wait a gosh darn second pop, hold on.

*(**GABBY** is really paying attention now.)*

FATHER. Listen *mijo*, listen.

*(We hear the lowest, deepest rumble like that of a tremor but more harmonic, churning as it moves through the house and is gone, **GABBY** jumps up like cat.)*

GABBY. I heard it! I heard it! Dad I heard it, I heard the monster.

*(**GABBY** takes quick jabs at **FATHER**'s raised hands. A quick celebration and then an embrace.)*

FATHER. Did you feel it *mijo*? Did you?

GABBY. I did, I did! I swear.

FATHER. That is the Power *mijo*, that is what you are to me.

*(***GABBY*** raise both arms showing cheerio muscles.)*

FATHER. (*whispering*) You are power.

*(Little ***GABBY*** trembles as though he is possessed.)*

GABBY. I! AM! POWER!!!

FATHER. That's right. And you will be a *sanjero* like Mister Moulholland!
Controlling the water valves of the Mother Ditch, La Sanja madre en Chinatown. You must never be what I am, *mijo*.

GABBY. A Mexican?

FATHER. A Mexican you will always be, with your head held high. A poor Mexican you will never be, I will make sure of it.

GABBY. But I wanna be just like you pop.

*(***FATHER*** pours himself a tequila. This bitter drink barely holds down the pain and hurt of a man who wanted more.)*

FATHER. I dig ditches boy! I dig ditches.
But you and Gilbert will be the men who decide where the water and the power come and go in this desert pueblo. One day if you're lucky, you will run the DWP!

GABBY. The Department of White People!!!

*(***DAD*** taps ***GABBY*** upside the back of the head.)*

FATHER. Here, drink this, quickly.

*(Father offers ***GABBY*** a small shot of tequila, ***GABBY*** drinks it with a sour lemon face.)*

FATHER. Shake it off *mijo*.

*(***GABBY*** shakes his head wildly.)*

FATHER. Now go clobber your brother in the head when he's not looking, *andale*!

GABBY. Gilbert, hurry up, dad wants us to rule the greater Los Angeles for the poor people and I don't want to be late!

*(***GABBY*** exits. ***FATHER*** proudly grabs his lunch box and exits.)*

FATHER. Fucking A right....

Scene Five

(NORTE/SUR makes his way to the stage.)

(He may wheel himself several feet across POWER.)

(POWER does not see or acknowledge him.)

(NORTE/SUR slowly punches the air.)

NORTE/SUR. Water.

(He brings up the other closed fist.)

Power.

Water for life. Power for progress.

(NORTE/SUR punctuates these words with gentle punches straight ahead.)

Water/Power.

(He opens a book.)

NORTE/SUR. This is my piece book, I keep all sorts of things in here. I did the cover myself. These are my poems, little stories, drawings and articles of interest. Oh, here goes my drawing of Snoopy in a lowrider. Pocahantas on a stripper pole. Yeah, gots all kinds of crazy stuff in here. I kinda keep a record of the things people want to forget.

Here's a newspaper picture of the night I got shot by Officer Garcia, Mister Power. That's my carnal right there, you can't really see me but those are my legs sticking out. If you look real close, you can see my Lucky Lugz aye, my lucky shoes. I always wore them lucky lugz when I ran the streets. Every homeboy & homegirl needs a little luck running those streets out there.

I was locked up in County with a Homeboy named Lucky, he's dead already. He didn't have permission to fly his own colors, so they beat him down, so I guess Lucky was unlucky. It just goes back and forth like that.

See, you're probably wondered why I called my shoes Lucky Lugz if I had them on both times I got shot. Well, I'm still alive ain't I?

Riddle me this: If you got invited to the best restaurant in LA would you feel lucky? I guess that would depend on who's picking up the tab.

(Enter **THE FIXER** *and* **WATER** *followed by the Fixer's Body Man* **EL MINISTRO**. *The* **FIXER** *is in an elegant white suit and is the power behind the most powerful in the City.* **EL MINISTRO** *wears a black suit and perhaps a black Turbin.* **EL MINISTRO** *always has iPod earphones in his ear holes.* **FIXER** *enters talking…)*

FIXER. Hey Champ, do you like having the Water Grill to yourself in the wee hours of the rainy morning? I like fusion. Do you like fusion? I'm just ravenous.

*(***BUS BOY*** with dear antlers enters and places the fancy* **WATER** *down.)*

FIXER. *Gracias. So,* Agua y Poder. Water, Power. Power, Water. Lefty loosey & righty tighty. Tell me, how are they? Out of the womb best friends. Los Carnales! Gosh, when was the last time I saw you? I remember, private box, Staples Center. Am I right? Who were you with that night? Ah yes! The powerful San Diego Councilman and the Orange County Sheriff. Lord, you was rolling mob deep that night. Chicanos swimming in the upper waters with the great white sharks. Before their impending indictments.

Funny thing you know, I was saying to an SC graduate ethics class just this morning how essential it is in our sometimes, unfortunate business to protect the sacred public trust. Trust. It is a precious commodity amigo.And if you trust me try that watercress salad there, it is divine.

WATER. No thank you.

FIXER. So, how's tricks? What can I do for my go getter – do gooder brothers Garcia? What does it say there in front of where your daddy used to work? Water for Life, Power for Progress. Does it still say that? I just love that. Makes me feel safe somehow. LA can still be a scary town you know.

WATER. Who ever this gentleman standing behind you is I need him to leave.

FIXER. He can't hear a thing. Relax.

WATER. I can't. I cannot relax.

(The FIXER looks over his shoulder to EL MINISTRO, he removes his ipod earphones.)

MINISTRO. Si jefe?

FIXER. Oh don't call me that, it embarrasses me so.

MINISTRO. Forgive me sir.

FIXER. What on earth are you listening to?

MINISTRO. The Notorious B.I.G.

FIXER. Ooh, I love them.

FIXER. Throw your signs in the air!
I just love that! So much raw power and truth in the rap game. Just breaking down the knowledge fool. I tried like hell to keep Biggie alive, damn. But I tell you Gilbert, *this* fella rolls correct or he don't roll at all.

MINISTRO. *Palabra.*

(EL MINISTRO taps his heart two times in the Pimp/ Playa way.)

FIXER. You know who gave me my street cred don't you? A certain Mister Tupac Shakur. Whom I met at the Playboy Mansion with his personal bodyguard, a moonlighting LAPD sergeant. Your brother. Who you need to keep alive.

WATER. So here's the deal...

FIXER. No. Here's the dealeo Senator Garcia, and please listen oh so carefully boo, the city doesn't need two more snot nosed Mexican kids sharing a prison cell with our good friends the Councilman and the Sheriff. La Pinta would be a very unpleasant place for a former star prosecutor and his cop brother. Nortenos and Surenos all swole from the iron pile, fighting over the twins. And here's the unfortunate kicker for you and your carnal: Four teams of shooters from Imperial Beach to Soledad all have the green light on Senor Poder. And you know what happens when Power lines hit the ground.

(Distant thunder cue echos in the distance.)

(The **BUS BOY** *delivers the white wine. The glasses are pre set.)*

FIXER. Thank you boo.

*(***WATER***'s Blackberry chirps.* **WATER** *looks at the time and shuts it off.)*

FIXER. Eat. You'll need it. Break Bread like the good Lord said. Treat yourself don't cheat yourself.

WATER. I have never asked you for anything. And tonight I need a favor.

FIXER. And I need a prison on the Eastside. Does not mean I'm going to get a prison on the eastside.

WATER. Gloria will never allow that to happen.

FIXER. I need condos on your LA River Green Space Mister Agua, I need live/work lofts, gated communities. Gringo hipsters walking little dogs, storefront galleries with crap-art, a Coffee Bean would be sa-weet! IKEA, East LA!

WATER. We are not having this conversation.

FIXER. We most certainly are.

WATER. Oh, I cannot...look, that land is going green.

FIXER. Didn't you get enough Greenpeace pussy during the "Heal The Bay" era?

WATER. My green bill is well on its way to the governor, sir.

FIXER. There are sundry ways a bill can die from committee to Terminator.

WATER. That land has been promised to the people. I gave my word.

FIXER. Nothing is concrete in LA, except the river.

WATER. I made a promise.

FIXER. The men looking for your carnal have a promise too.

WATER. My gosh is this is a shakedown, sir?

FIXER. Heavens no, I'm trying to square-deal-ya' here amigo.

WATER. Well then for God sake ask anything else of me I am prepared to offer you anything else. Just please, please, please, help me make my brother's safety a reality.

FIXER. Is there even a contexto for reality here? I mean step through this slowly with me senator: top ranking cop bivouacked at seedy motel with side kick crippled cholo. Well dressed assassins on Officer Garcia's trail, Cops on Officer Garcia's trail. Prison gang, who's name – so feared – I dare not repeat it at this table, donning War Bonnets as we speak. Might I suggest we bow our heads and pray to my good friend the Cardinal that nobody find Officer Garcia before I can work my miracle.

WATER. I came here to seek your good council because of the tremendous amount of respect I have for you. Not to bargain with you.

FIXER. You don't fuck with La Eme!!

You don't fuck with La Eme boo, boo. If you wanna walk across hot coals with Tony Robbins? Passé but okay. Rolling brown outs in unincorporated sections of the San Fernando Valley just for kicks, cool, a BJ from a better class of lips you got it.

I can make the bells ring three times at any firehouse in LA and all that happy shit if you desire but don't come asking me to help the poor bastard who kills a top soldier from the other team as an independent contractor? My gosh! I've got no wiggle room here Gib's.

PD brass got their blue panties in a bunch in record time on this one. La Eme won't come to the table unless I let them go tea bags on my forehead and I'm just getting to old for that shit. El Hermano has fucked up big time. He may in fact already reside in that special place juuuust outside my reach.

WATER. Nothing is out of your reach.

FIXER. I can't reach the salt. Pass it. Soup to nuts my boy, soup to nuts. It's a package deal.

(**FIXER** *pours wine.*)

FIXER. Drink your fine South African Riesling councilor, after all, Chinese children may be dying of thirst in Orange County tonight.

Salvation of the soul, protection of the body. You're sweating, champ. Never let tem see your precipitation kid.

(**WATER** *proceeds with caution and calculation.*)

WATER. Did you ever see a Mezuzah's in an East Los Angeles doorway? I have. In Boyle Heights. And it struck me you know, one culture stepping into the footprints of another. And all these Mexican families moving into these East-side homes protected by this wonderful little thing up there, in the doorway. I had no idea what it was at first. But one of Fred Ross' old time volunteers explained it to me. And I never forgot. You worked with Fred once upon a time. Way back when. When he and Saul trained a kid named Cesar Chavez. You were *there*. And now The Cesar Chavez River Walk Way will honor all of that. It is a beautiful piece of legislation. Essential. This bill is my Mezuzah for the eastside.

FIXER. Have I heard you tell that story before?

WATER. Lest we forget where we came from.

FIXER. Don't sit here and act like you haven't sucked on the perky titties of entitlement, Gilbert. The Twins have exploited every pink nipple of opportunity ever presented to them. Ambition. Tis your American right, like daddy's G.I. Bill, so lets be clear, this is why we find ourselves at this table tonight. Everything is on the table amigo. You and I are the modern long knives, and we must continue to carve up the eastside. I need one more slice of the Brier Patch.

WATER. What else? What else can this humble public servant do for you sir?

FIXER. Kill your bill in committee, senator.

WATER. Absolutely not.

FIXER. You're tougher than the mothers of East L.A.

WATER. My people want clean air too.

FIXER. Do I give a fuck? Ooh! Idea: how 'bout I get the construction companies who have contributed to all your campaigns to build a computer center for the Chicanitos? The Cesar Chavez Education Center, between an Olive Garden and a Forever 21!

WATER. It won't wash. Political suicide.

FIXER. LA loves a stimulus package. Your constituents will forgive you.

WATER. Chicanos don't forgive. It's not in our DNA.

FIXER. They wouldn't throw the baby out with the bath water...

WATER. *La Llorona* comes to mind.

FIXER. Look boo, the Brothers Garcia have managed to piss off some very powerful people.

WATER. One of the brothers.

FIXER. We don't discern where one brother leaves off and the other begins, after all, I'm just a stupid white guy from Brentwood so what do I know?

WATER. Why don't you save your "just a white guy from Brentwood" routine for your pedophilic clients at the Arch Diocese.

FIXER. Come here. Come. Lean in. Let me tell you what this white guy knows that you may not. And I can only say this once, so follow the bouncing ball as best you can Gilbert. The badass hombre your brother assassinated in East Los Angeles earlier this evening was carrying a contract for murder of a high profile target.

That "contract" was signed, sealed and approved by a commission of men, hombres whose very existence I know scarcely about. And I know a lot. I know this: the contract – due to the death of badass hombre – killed by the hand of your brother is now null and void, nobody can carry it out. Having said that, there is this caveat, the new improved contract transfers to Power.

WATER. I don't follow.

FIXER. Neither did I. I had to look it up. Real spick-y stuff, archaic rules going back to your old country. In effect, your brother – by his actions – so egregious – exchanged his name for the original on the contract.

WATER. Who was the original target?

(Pointing his elegant finger with near silent power. True power.)

FIXER. You. Remember an over zealous, ambitious prosecutor named Gilbert Garcia? He sent a nobody street thug named Escobar, to prison 12 years ago for a crime he did not commit. Officer Garcia and his boys altered all police reports and evidence naturally. Mr. Nobody became Mr. Somebody who was released yesterday. Mr. Somebody had the green light to pull off the first known hit on a sitting member of the California State Senate. Your twin brother stopped history. Contrails of corruption every which way. Your hermano saved your life. And now you must save his. My condos.

WATER. Not possible.

FIXER. Hate the game not the player. This is LA boycheck, anything is possible. For example: I ask PD to stand down while this fellow and his brother from Culiacan...

MINISTRO. Matamoros.

FIXER. I stand corrected. Matamoros. He and his brother, will be at the Motel Paradise in forty two minutes to pick up all unauthorized LAPD weapons and sweep the place of various narcotics. The brothers will then plant those weapons on an expendable homeboy in the city of...Carson! Sometime between now and let's say sunrise.

And do let me know when our ribbon cutting ceremony can commence on that lush water way we forgivingly call the LA River. I can see the gondoliers already. Rowing never drifting.

Gilbert, I cannot stress enough how important it is that everything outlined this evening proceed in a timely fashion. Any deviation could be most unpleasant Senator?

(beat)

WATER. Okay.

FIXER. Make the call Gilbert. Gods not looking. Green space dies. Power lives. Be a game changer champ. Who lives, who dies, once again, the Jewish Storytellers.

(WATER reaches for his Blackberry and hits the speed dial.)

WATER. Hey guy, uh, shit, listen, we've hit a brick wall, they, uh, we have found toxin's on the land, and some sort of Indian burial ground as well. Chumash I think. I have to kill the bill. Calm down, calm down. I know, it's a certified shit-sandwich.

Listen carefully, lets leak some of Bob's shady finance stuff with that developer to the press, I gotta swift boat this mother fucker before he does me. Yup. The Green Space is dead. It's a Brown Field and we're waking away now. Go.

*(**WATER** makes his way back to the table and gulps down wine and a few pills from the Oxycontin med bottle from the motel room.)*

FIXER. All in all I'd say a very productive evening. Good work, son.

WATER. Fuck the whores of this town.

FIXER. *(almost sweet)* But you are one of us. You know Rabbi Learner says we must all endeavor to be happy, it is our responsibility, takes real effort though. I don't like a young man who does not dream. The City still needs your dreams kid. She hungers for them.

*(**WATER** drinks directly from the white wine bottle.)*

(There is another thunder.)

FIXER. Your Mezuzah story. The late, great, Honorable Edward R. Roybal told that story much better, rest in peace.

*(**FIXER** crosses himself.)*

FIXER. He told it much better because it was his story. Not yours. As hard as you try champ I just don't see a *Yamulka* on your brown head.

Alas, the hour is late, we forget things. I used to deliver the Herald Examiner in City Terrace at this exact time. Lord I've been on these old tires all day. I usually enjoy a foot massage in tepid water about this time but my masseuse has retired for the night sadly.

*(The **DEER DANCER**/**BUS BOY** returns with a small wash basin. **WATER** rises from his chair as **EL MINISTRO** moves the table away.)*

FIXER. Would you wash my feet in warm salted water, Water?

WATER. That's hilarious.

FIXER. I need for you to wash my feet in warm salted water.

WATER. The fuck you say…

*(The **ANTLER/BUS BOY** places a foot towel on the floor for the **FIXER** and poors warm water and then the salt.)*

FIXER. Water and Power. Power and Water, they thought they were real Princes of the City, the Dukes of Earl, but they're still just snot-nosed Mexican kids from the eastside dripping down daddies leg.

*(**EL MINISTRO** hangs quiet and menacingly in the shadows.)*

*(The **FIXER** methodically places his feet in the basin.)*

FIXER. Ah, nothing more soothing in the world. Come. Don't be shy or embarrassed, I had to do this a hundred times before I got the hang of it.

*(Silence and the sound of water as the **ANTLER/BUS BOY** scoops water. with his hands and washes the **FIXER**'s feet.)*

FIXER. Just listen to that water. That's it. Come closer Water, come to the water, man.

*(**EL MINISTRO** moves in and carefully removes **WATER**'s jacket, gently nudging **WATER** toward the basin. **MINISTRO** steps back as **WATER** knows what he must do, he goes to his knees like in church. Each beat is methodical. The **DEER DANCER** steps away a few feet.)*

FIXER. I have always maintained, contrary to popular belief and medical certainty that water, is in fact thicker than blood.

*(**WATER** reaches into the basin and begins to wash the **FIXER**'s feet.)*

FIXER. Good Hispanic, good Hispanic. Good.
Easy there. Oh, you're feeling me now, dawg.
What's the take away here Gibs? What did we learn tonight?
You're doing it like a white man now kid.

(WATER looks up to the DEER DANCER, the boy turns away. WATER glances to the audience right and left, this is pure humiliation, we/audience are his witness.)

FIXER. Barak Obama has beautiful feet!
God I love this town. How does that song go?
I love LA...
Sixth Street, I love it! Crenshaw, I love it!
South Central.....I love it! Hawaiian Gardens! I live it...

(Lights down on the FIXER.)

Scene Seven

(Back at the Motel Paradise: **POWER** *his pointing his gun into the mirror sort of posing for* **NORTE/SUR**. **NORTE/SUR** *who is hunched over his piece book drawing fast. The radio is on.)*

POWER. Just like this, calm like a bomb.

NORTE/SUR. Hold still man, almost done. Raise your arm just a bit homes.

POWER. Any higher and it's not what I did. It will be your version of what I did. Not what I really did.

NORTE/SUR. You're talking to the Picasso of the Barrio homes. Got it.

*(***NORTE/SUR** *closes the piece book,* **POWER** *relaxes his pose. A beat.)*

POWER. It's real quiet. Damn. I hate when it gets this quiet.

*(***NORTE/SUR** *looks at his watch.)*

NORTE/SUR. How long's your *carnal* been gone?

POWER. A few hours.

NORTE/SUR. How much did you tell him?

POWER. Not everything. Turn the radio up man.

*(***NORTE/SUR** *wheels over and turns on a small radio. We hear a song come over the radio.)*

POWER. Ah man, I love this jam. Damn. Oh yeah. Must be the Huggie Boy show.

*(***POWER** *takes the center of the motel room and really feels and takes in the slow jam. He lifts his arms the way the homeboys do when they dance.)*

POWER. Ah yeah, feel it homes.

NORTE/SUR. I remember this dance aye, its been a while but I remember dancing with the *jainas*. Sha!

(From his chair **NORTE/SUR** *starts to dance using his arms. The cop and the cholo are dancing to the oldie.)*

POWER. Do it right or don't do it at all, homeboy.

NORTE/SUR. Orale.

(**POWER** *goes behind* **NORTE/SUR** *wheelchair and gently lifts him from behind, holding him up* **POWER** *provides the legs and feet for the crippled cholo.*)

POWER. There it is right there. You got it bro.

NORTE/SUR. Don't let your bro hear you call me bro.

POWER. Don't trip. Just feel the music man.

NORTE/SUR. I remember dancing just like this.

POWER. Yeah?

NORTE/SUR. Not with a cop right behind me but something like this.

POWER. Been a long time since I danced like this.

NORTE/SUR. Is it hard to dance when killers are looking for you?

POWER. It's the best time to dance.

NORTE/SUR. I gotta write that one down ese.

POWER. Don't write, just dance. Feel the jam.

NORTE/SUR. Hey man, is that your night stick in my ass or has it just been a long time since you danced with a *cholo.*

POWER. Shut the fuck up man.

(**POWER** *sort of tosses* **NORTE/SUR** *on the bed.* **NORTE/ SUR** *reaches for his book and pulls his chair close to him.* **POWER** *keeps moving to the jam.*)

NORTE/SUR. Hey *vato*, if anything happens to you, you know like something bad, and you die and shit, don't hang around like Patrick Swayze did in that movie.

POWER. I'll be long gone, trust me.

NORTE/SUR. I'll see to it that even the homies come by to pay their respects to Power, know what I mean?

POWER. You would do that for me?

NORTE/SUR. Homey love. For sure.

(**NORTE/SUR** *back makes his way back in his chair. One of his legs needs help back into the chair.*)

NORTE/SUR. Help me with my left foot *ese?*

POWER. Daniel Day Lewis over here.

NORTE/SUR. In the Name of the Father.

POWER. Don't change the subject, which homeboys, which ones will come to my cop wake?

NORTE/SUR. Uh, I don't know, I'd have to check it out you know, see which *vatos* are available, I 'm sure I could dig up somebody.

(**POWER** *likes the idea.*)

POWER. Hey, get the hardcore vatos from White Fence or *Cuatro* Flats, OG's, *veteranos* from the old school. No youngsters.

NORTE/SUR. I dunno ese, the older OG'S are kinda busy with funerals and shit

POWER. So which homeys from <u>LA</u> can you get for sure?

NORTE/SUR. Well, I know at least one fake ass *cholo* from Silverlake who might come. He wears a Von Dutch hat backwards but I'll make sure he takes it off when he comes to the wake.

POWER. No hipsters at my funeral. And that's an order.

NORTE/SUR. I'll find someone. Come hell or high water.

POWER. Just forget it.

NORTE/SUR. Maybe I could get Edward James Olmos to come, I helped him sweep the streets after the LA Riots, he owes me.

(**POWER** *slowly points his gun at* **NORTE/SUR. NORTE/ SUR** *writes a note.*)

NORTE/SUR. No Edward James Olmos.

Scene Eight

(Transition: **NORTE/SUR** *exits the motel. The* **DEER DANCER** *moves slowly through the hotel room.* **POWER** *moves about with his AK47, not seeing or relating to the* **DEER DANCER.** **NORTE/SUR** *speaks from an isle/corridor leading to the stage.)*

NORTE/SUR. Do you see the Deer Dancer there? If you do, you are one of the lucky ones. He is our protection, a lucky charm, a talisman. I first saw him at McCarthur Park in LA, dancing with the Elders, so I know he comes from a long line of Deer Dancers. His people came from across the Rio Yaqui, a familia known as the Clan of the Wolf. Even on these mean streets of LA, one whispers those words: Clan of The Wolf. *Los Fariceos.* They wore baggie black pants, black shoes, white tee's and black shirts buttoned only at the top like the homey's do. They were the first known cholos. Like real gangsters. This little vato came from all that.

This little Deer Dancer vato must dance ceremony all night, if he stumbles or falls, if the cops kick his ass, if he stops dancing, then nothing can keep the Lords of Death away from the Killing Floor at The Motel Paradise.

This little vato was taught that death in the Big City is imminent, and every little Deer Dancer knows that his dance ends in death, but he must continue on the Red Road regardless. He must dance so that others can live. You never get something for nothing.

(**NORTE/SUR** *exits the stage as we:)*

Scene Nine

(Transition back to Motel Paradise. 4am. Enter **WATER**.*)*

POWER. Bagpipes. I want bagpipes. You be sure I have them.

WATER. What?

POWER. Yeah. We play them across the street when we bury cops.

WATER. We don't have time for this, man.

POWER. I've lost a lot of brothers already. The politicians change, you guys come and go, but the bagpipes remain.

*(***POWER** *points toward the cathedral.)*

POWER. There.

(pointing to his head)

POWER. Here. Bagpipes. Damn, I hate the feeling of power they give me. So real you know?

WATER. We'll talk in the car, let's go.

POWER. Rows and rows of cops, sheriffs from all over the country. Standing at attention in the cathedral court-yard for hours in the hot sun. Nobody moving out of reverence for a fallen brother. Patrol cars lined up from here to Chinatown. Engine ladders crossed, the flag hanging over Temple and Grand Avenue.

Carefully fold the flag that was draped over the coffin, pass it to the widow. She is weary of our remembrance faces.

Sometimes the child of a Fallen Officer is so young they think every cop is their father. What do you say to that, bro? What do you tell that child?

So I ask my God Cop in my best white voice: what do you want from me? And I make my little deals with him. He wants me to take my grief and turn it into power. That power is the bullets coming out of my sidearm. It's the baton crashing down on the next cleanly shaven head. My God is righteous, bro. And righteous are the Peace-keepers. I am a monster, but he forgives me because I am a monster built of dead cops and bagpipes. They built this Dark House. One cop funeral at a time.

WATER. You don't have to justify your bagpipes and your choirboy bullshit to me, bro. I made the deal.

POWER. I didn't ask you to make a fucking deal. What did you give up?

WATER. A lot.

POWER. You stupid fuck. You didn't have to do that.

WATER. Oh I did.

POWER. Why are you always trying to be the good guy?

WATER. I've heard the bagpipes.

POWER. The smart brother?

WATER. I heard them at the cathedral.

POWER. Why the fuck are you always trying to save the goddamned world Gil?

WATER. We were taught to save the goddamned world, Gabe. Do you remember that? That is what we were taught. And I *have* heard your bagpipes bro, and they weren't for one of your cops, no, bagpipes mixed with the voices of farm workers. Bagpipes for Cesar, Gabe.

POWER. Cesar who?

WATER. Chavez!

POWER. Fuck Cesar.

WATER. Never say that again, Gabe. We made a promise to Cesar and that is what I gave up tonight for you.

POWER. For you!

WATER. For you, bro! For dad.

POWER. Fuck dad, fuck Cesar, fuck all promises made to anybody anywhere!

(**POWER** *raises his pistol toward his brother.*)

POWER. And fuck your *De Colores.* Your bagpipes are not my bagpipes.

WATER. Gabby, man, put the gun down bro. Listen to me, please.

POWER. I can't hear you, the bagpipes drown you out.

WATER. Put the gun down.

POWER. You want to hear De Colores? Fine, you sing it. Remind me of that tune, hum a few bars, c'mon bitch sing it! Sing it!

(**POWER** *slams the magazine into the revolver.* **WATER**
goes to his knees. Turbine sounds begin.)

POWER. Sing it motherfucker, sing your goddamn song Cesar!

(**POWER** *cocks gun.* **WATER** *pleads with his brother but
struggles to find the words, to make a sound.*)

WATER. Please, Gabe.

(**POWER** *takes aim.*)

WATER. *De Colores, De Colores se visten los campos in la prima-
vera...*

POWER. Yeah, sing it!

WATER. *De Colores, de Colores...*

POWER. Next verse, keep going, come on, sing Cesar, sing!

WATER. *...los pajarillos...*

POWER. Sing! Sing!

WATER. That's all I know! I don't remember all the words.

POWER. *(menacing whisper)* You phony Hispanic fuck. You
got played tonight. Beg like a white man.

(**POWER** *laughs wildly.* **WATER** *tackles* **POWER** *in that
moment.*)

(*There is a struggle, the gun falls to the floor. The brothers are wrestling, more struggle.*)

(*Turbines can be heard.*)

(*The wrestling turns into an all out fist fight and a
struggle for the loaded gun. Punches are thrown and the
brothers go down.*)

(*Suddenly the lights go out. Silence.*)

POWER. Quiet. Quiet Gibby.

WATER. Huh?

POWER. Hear that?

WATER. What?

(*Then a surge of turbine like a short tremor and then
ground to a halt.*)

(*On another part of the stage we see* **NORTE/SUR.**)

Scene Ten – The Dark House

(**NORTE/SUR** *wheels across the stage in the darkness.*)

NORTE/SUR. <u>The Dark House</u>. This Dark House shit is for real dog. I'm very, very serious right now. Maybe because I'm afraid of the dark myself, don't tell nobody, its private information. Let me ask you this. Have you ever been in a place so dark that you can't tell if you're alone in space or surrounded by monsters?

I've been in the Dark House before. Yeah, there was a *cholo* carnival in the hood, and my homey had just OD'd on the Zipper, *se murio* right there, so I went into the funhouse so nobody could see me cry. It was so dark in there, man, I couldn't find my way out for two hours. I was real scared. Those Lords of Death were reaching for me, smiling all happy through sad clown faces in the blackness. Endless.

I read somewhere that the Maya got so tripped out in the pitch black jungles of the Yucatan, that they left without a trace.

Watcha' ma call it, the Bro's have been kicked to the Dark House by the Lords of Death, and the bro's are throwing blows now. Ambitious *vatos*, smart guys, hopefully they can figure out what so many cannot.

(*voice of a child:*)

CHILD. (*offstage*) *Power, come out and play-yay. Power, come out and play-yay…*

Scene Eleven – Back at the Motel

(*The brothers are still in the dark.*)

POWER. Gibby? Gibby?

WATER. What?

POWER. You okay?

WATER. Fuck off.

(*huge thunder then lightning*)

WATER/POWER. Woah!!!

WATER. How the hell was there just lightening after the Thunder?

POWER. Because that was the Thunder after the last lightening from before.

WATER. Sounds about right.

POWER. You stuck me pretty good, *carbon.*

WATER. Should have taken your fucking head off man.

(*Lightning*)

WATER. Damn, stop.

POWER. You escared?

WATER. Yeah.

POWER. You always hated thunder, since you we were little.

WATER. Yep.

POWER. Remember that time when we were camping and the tent got flooded and there were bears and Indians and stuff?

WATER. Nope. You obviously have our childhood mixed up with somebody else's.

POWER. Yeah, I saw it on Scooby Doo.

(**POWER** *cracks himself up like a motherfucker.*)

WATER. You could have told me my name was on the contract? You're a real jerk you know that?

POWER. Was that really all you knew of *de Colores*?

WATER. Yeah, I'm a phony fuck, remember?

POWER. Sing it again. Maybe it will come back to you

WATER. It won't.

POWER. *Si se puede.*

WATER. Stop.

POWER. Please bro, I'm begging on my knees.

WATER. You're not on your knees you're sitting on your fat ass.

POWER. C'mon

WATER. Ah right, *la Gallina con el pio, pio, pio*, there's a bunch more *pios* ...

(beat)

Then a Flock of Seagulls...and...She's buying a stairway to heaven...

(In an instant **NORTE/SUR** *is in the Motel Room.)*

NORTE/SUR. *Y por eso los grandes amores de muchos colores me gustan a mi!)*

(Thunder. Lights flicker on.)

NORTE/SUR. Am I the only mother fucker up in here that knows the words to *De Colores?* While you two were rolling around in here I wheeled myself up to Lilac Terrace. I get a good view from up there, coyotes howling and everything.

WATER. And?

NORTE/SUR. Well, word on the street is this: "no contract" on Power. The homeys are standing down. Nobody's *tirando* blows against you now.

POWER. I'm not buying it. Nobody's got *that* much power.

NORTE/SUR. *Te lo juro* homey.

WATER. I told you it's done, it's handled. With *my* guy.

(Sounds of helicopters. **POWER** *swings into action.)*

POWER. It's never done. I don't know *your* guy, I don't trust *your* guy.

*(***NORTE/SUR** *lays out new weapons, mostly small hand guns on the dresser, he begins to load them.)*

WATER. Gabe, Gabe?

POWER. No. They're coming here man, and they are gonna take me out, they don't miss.

NORTE/SUR. Maybe you should get out of here right now Water man. Take this and go.

(Handing him a weapon. **POWER** *intercepts the side arm.)*

POWER. No. Just go bro, go, you can't help me now.

WATER. I did help you. I'm part of the deal now.

POWER. There is no deal. It's a set up! This ain't your game Gilbert. I told you, no code, no rules, I'm out man. It's that simple.

WATER. It's not going down like that.

POWER. The men who are coming here are going to kill me.

WATER. *La Eme* isn't coming here bro.

POWER. I'm not talking about *La Eme.*

WATER. You got it wrong bro. I'm taking you home. LAPD is part of the fucking package.

POWER. Does Contagious Fire mean anything to you?

WATER. My guy's got LAPD in check.

POWER. LA's better off without me.

WATER. They're going to arrest another soldier for the murder. No. We're walking. That's the deal, that's the promise. See those guys in the parking lot?

NORTE/SUR. The *vatos* in the Crown Vic?

WATER. No, the black Escalade.

NORTE/SUR. When did they roll up?

WATER. Just now. Those are *my* guys, we're golden.

(**POWER** *peeks out the window.*)

POWER. Traffic Division is closing down part of Sunset.

WATER. Your city is working, that's all.

POWER. Norte/Sur?

NORTE/SUR. Sounds like it could be but I just don't know for sures. Difficult to be certain.

POWER. What should I do homey?

WATER. Hey, I'm right here and I'm telling you what to do homey.

POWER. Give us just a moment bro. Please?

(**NORTE/SUR** *has to move past* **WATER** *toward* **POWER.**)

NORTE/SUR. *Despensa* homes.

WATER. Right. I'm not in your car.

(*We hear a Harley Davidson drive by in the distance:*)

NORTE/SUR. *(more of question to himself)* That sounded like *Rafas.*

(**POWER** *crouches close to* **NORTE/SUR,** *they hold hands in a soul handshake way. It is a quiet, intimate moment.* **WATER** *looks away.*)

POWER. What do I do?

NORTE/SUR. This is for sure some critical shit right here, Gabe. Maybe Water has it like that with his fixe*r vato.*

POWER. Maybe, huh?

NORTE/SUR. What's plan B aye?

POWER. *(grave)* Got a pair of dice?

NORTE/SUR. I heard some other foo's were gonna die tonight for sure. Word had come down from the penitentiary like that you know. *(snap of the fingers)* The *vatos* were gonna dust some black dudes in The Avenues that had nothing to do with this *pedo.* Blame it on the *mayates* again and shit. It ain't right homey.

POWER. Lawless Avenues.

NORTE/SUR. Its the Wild Wild West homey. You messed with the Chain of Command *vato.* And unless I'm very wrong, and if Water's *vato* doesn't have *that* kind of power, then...

POWER. ...the worst is yet to come.

NORTE/SUR. Let me ask you this: what does your Spidey Sense tell you?

POWER. To be ready for anything.

NORTE/SUR. Then ask your brother to put something on it.

WATER. I'm right here Norte/Sur, talk to me.

NORTE/SUR. For the safety of your *carnal,* for the Brothers, put something on it.

WATER. I already put a million trees on it so fuck you Norte/Sur.

NORTE/SUR. Good point.

(**NORTE/SUR** *looks back to* **POWER.**)

NORTE/SUR. I'm gonna have to go with your carnal on this one aye. You must accept Water's terms. Either that or go out in a blaze of glory. Like a cholo on the 4th of July.

(**POWER** *leans into* **NORTE/SUR.**)

POWER. He's been telling me what to do my whole life man, I just thought tonight it would be my turn to call the shots. The shotcaller.

NORTE/SUR. I hear you bro, but then again why switch up now, of all nights you know?

POWER. Yeah.

NORTE/SUR. And the sooner the better so we can end this *desmadre.*

WATER. It's over. It's over guys. We're leaving all weapons behind. I'm gonna pack you up myself bro. Norte/ Sur, please roll out to the parking lot and tell black Escalade we're coming out in two minutes. You're the signal they're waiting for.

NORTE/SUR. *Simon.*

WATER. And ask them how fast they can get to Cedar's emergency room just in case…

(Just before **NORTE/SUR** *exits he faces* **POWER** *who is seated at the edge of the bed.)*

NORTE/SUR. This feels right.

*(***NORTE/SUR** *begins to move out.)*

NORTE/SUR. Stay up foo.

POWER. Stay down dawg.

(They touch knuckles.)

WATER. Go!

NORTE/SUR. Gone.

*(***NORTE/SUR** *wheels out to the parking lot. The brothers are left together.)*

WATER. Gabe? Gabe?

(beat)

POWER. Let's do it then.

*(***WATER** *starts gathering* **POWER** *'s things and moves into the john,* **POWER** *sits on the edge of the bed.)*

POWER. I'm sorry bro, Sorry about all this.

*(***WATER** *keeps moving to pack up his brother.)*

WATER. We'll get through it lieutenant, you'll see, we'll take a vacation together, go away for a while you know, head up the coast, spank whitey at Pebble Beach maybe. Relax. And this long night will be behind us soon enough bro. Shit, dad might even have been proud of us.

POWER. Yeah.

WATER. Shoot, Dad might even have been proud of us.

POWER. You think?

WATER. Golly yeah, proud of his Water and Power-man.

(*The twins embrace*)

POWER. You 've always been the Shotcaller bro.

WATER. Rainmaker bro. It's the way dad wanted it I guess.

POWER. Yeah. Go clean your face Senator. You got a little something right there.

(**WATER** *goes to the head to wash up.*)

(**POWER** *begins to quietly lay out the Black Tarpaulin on the Motel Bed. Lights down as* **FATHER** *and a young* **POWER/GABBY** *enter singing De Colores.*)

(*Little* **POWER** *is on his dad's shoulders.* **DAD** *carries his Sir Guy jacket.*)

(*The men are dressed nice and stand if front of the old D.W.P. building #32 on Cahuenga Boulevard.*)

FATHER AND SON. ...*Y por ese los grandes amores,*
De muchos colores
Me gustan a mi.
Sing it mijo!

(**GABBY** *belts out the last verse con gusto.*)

GABBY. ...*Y por ese los grandes amores,*
De muchos colores
Me gustan a mi!!

FATHER. *Que bueno mijo!* The girls are gonna love it when you sing that song *mijo*.

GABBY. They all like Gilbert dad, I have bad luck with girls.

FATHER. I thought you were playing stink-finger with the little *gavachita* down the street?)

GABBY. Stink Finger?

FATHER. When you get older son, I want you to spread your seed all over LA. And never, ever, use a rubber.

GABBY. OK dad.

*(**GABBY** looks down.)*

FATHER. Where's your confiansa lil' Power man?

GABBY. I dunno. I'm a loser pop.

FATHER. No mijo, no. That's not true.

GABBY. Sure it is. Everybody calls me Eddie Munster. Its okay, I'm used to it.

FATHER. Haven't I learned you real good like your brother?

*(**GABBY** shrugs. Pop reaches to hug the wounded son.)*

FATHER. *Lo siento mijo, lo siento* son. Come here. I'm so sorry lil' man. I let you down. It's my fault *mijo.*

*(**FATHER** looks deep into his son's eyes.)*

FATHER. Never feel less than Gilbert. Ever.

GABBY. *(softly)* No?

FATHER. Golly no. He just gets lucky sometimes but you're tougher.

GABBY. I am?

FATHER. Lookie here lil *vato*, here is what we'll do. I'll be your sponsor.

GABBY. My sponsor?

FATHER. Like a look out. Your buddy. See *mijo*, we'll iron your brand new Chinos perfectly, like mine. And then, you can borrow my Sir Guy jacket. What you wanna do is carry it like a *vato*, a real gentleman. Never worn, always carried on your arm *a si.*

(Pop carefully wraps his jacket over his forearm cool like that)

GABBY. Wow, that's sharp dad. *Te vez muy* cool.

FATHER. No matters if your parents are on relief, man your stuff better look sharp. No excuses. And make sure those French Toes are spit shined but good.

*(**FATHER** does a cool pose. Chinos. Jacket. Shoes.)*

GABBY. Ooh.

FATHER. Here, you try.

(**GABBY** *drapes the Sir Guy jacket over his little arm and poses.*)

GABBY. *Orale.*

(Father and son do the secret handshake.)

FATHER. Outstanding *mijo.* Never worn, always carried. Chinos. Jacket. Shoes. The holy trinity.

(Dad does a nifty move running his hand thru his shiny hair. Father holds his hand out, palm up and lightly leans back.)

(**GABBY** *smells the brilliantine in his hand. He smiles to the high heavens, eyes closed. This is* **GABBY**'s *best day in the whole wide world.)*

GABBY. Hee, hee…

FATHER. Now go practice in the mirror. *Andale.*

(Little **GABBY** *runs from this area directly to the Motel Paradise, he is face to face with his grown up self.* **POWER** *is sitting on the plastic he just laid down. We hear* **WATER** *from the bathroom.)*

WATER. Hey, the water just went out.

(Little **GABBY** *speaks to older* **POWER**. *Himself.)*

GABBY. Dad says never wear your Sir Guy Jacket, just carry it like a vato.

POWER. Neat. Let's not tell Gilbert, okay.

GABBY. Okay.

POWER. Hey, you wanna get some chocolate cake later?

(Little **GABBY** *nods yes.* **POWER** *and his little self do a lovely little hand motion as if looking into a mirror.)*

WATER. You talking to yourself?

GABBY/POWER. Yeah.

GABBY. Is there a monster <u>under</u> the bed?

(**POWER** *nods no.)*

GABBY. Is there a monster <u>on</u> the bed?

POWER. The lady in the door way tonight, why did she look at me like that?

*(Little **GABBY** shrugs.)*

POWER. Did we kill mom when we were born?

GABBY. Dad says we're never supposed to talk about that.

POWER. Okay.

*(**POWER** slowly puts gun to head. **GABBY** runs off.)*

WATER. You say something bro?

POWER. Sorry what I said about Cesar.

(Click and white light:)

*(In the instant that **POWER** pulls back the hammer of the gun white light is on him at the edge of the bed – the click of the gun triggers the lights. These are not outside lights coming through the window or "people" closing in on **POWER**, this is **POWER** closing in on power. The lights are from inside the room.)*

(BOOM!)

*(**WATER** comes running in from the bathroom.)*

WATER. Gabby! No, Gabby. No. Norte/Sur!
Officer Down! Officer Down! Move it! Move it!

*(**WATER** cradles his brother from behind.)*

WATER. *(quiet)* Gabby!

(POLICE RADIO DISPATCH VOICE: FEMALE:)

OFFICER DOWN, 13 HUNDRED BLOCK OF WEST SUNSET BLVD...

*(5am. **POWER** is dead at the Motel Paradise. We hear a harder, urban version of the song from scene seven.)*

*(**WATER** cradles **POWER**. Holding his brothers head, **WATER** closes **POWER**'s eyes.)*

*(The bed moves upstage. **EL MINISTRO** quickly sweeps the room of weapons and furniture.)*

*(The **DEER DANCER** appears. He wears only the antlers, white peasant pants and ankle shakers. He carries another shaker.)*

*(**DEER DANCER**'s dance is an offering for the life of*

POWER *the dance becomes ever faster and forceful.)*

(The **DEER DANCER** *must dance with all his might to keep the Lords of Death at bay.)*

(The Lords of Death are receiving **POWER.** *)*

*(***DEER DANCER** *leaps for his life and exits.)*

(Sound of rain.)

Scene 12 – A Box of Rain

(NORTE/SUR enters. He wheels himself to a position on stage, he slowly looks up, arms stretched out, palms up. It rains down on NORTE/SUR. This box of rain is contained only for NORTE/SUR. Down pour. NORTE/SUR smells the rain. Feels the ceremony. He looks up to the sky.)

NORTE/SUR. I like the sound of the helicopters.

I like the way they feel.

The helicopters in the hood, ghetto birds flying low to the ground, sometimes so low I can feel the wind of their blades.

The power of their blades. It's the only breeze that day.

I can smell the jet fuel.

It's the only time I can feel the bones in my dead legs.

(NORTE/SUR begins to wheel out.)

NORTE/SUR. Ese Power!

(NORTE/SUR is cleansed. He continues to exit. Transition.)

(The stage is clean.)

(A MAN in rose hills overall's mops the small pool of WATER.)

(An indentation in the floor suggest a grave of POWER.)

(Bagpipes for POWER. Finally. Bagpipes flood the theater.)

(WATER enters in sport coat and sunglasses holding a single rose and placing it on POWER's grave. Bagpipes subside.)

(Enter NORTE/SUR.)

NORTE/SUR. Hey.

WATER. Hey.

(NORTE/SUR joins WATER at the graveside.)

WATER. Found the place all right?

NORTE/SUR. Took 18 buses to get here. A new record for me. Man, the Calvary Hill over there was a motherfucker.

WATER. Thanks for coming.

NORTE/SUR. So, how you doing?

WATER. I haven't seen you since that time at Trader Joes....

NORTE/SUR. Whole Foods ese. I saw you at Whole Foods not Trader Joe's. The aisles are wider at Whole Foods, I take note of that stuff.

WATER. I stand corrected.

NORTE/SUR. Full disclosure you know.

WATER. Due diligence my man. How are you?

NORTE/SUR. Real good, real good senator. We had a car wash for your brother you know, washed a lot of cop cars but hardly no *pedo,* all the homey's we're rolling tight out of respect for Mister Power's.

WATER. Good. Good.

NORTE/SUR. Damn, been over a month, still seems like yesterday. I really, really miss your carnal.

WATER. I know you do Norte/Sur.

NORTE/SUR. I miss, his, his noise you know? *Vato* made a lot of noise.

WATER. He did.

NORTE/SUR. I brought these flowers for him, they look kinda fucked up but at least I didn't steal them off another grave like the Armenians do.

(**NORTE/SUR** *looks around the cemetery.*)

NORTE/SUR. Gosh darn, takes a grip of water to make these cemetery's green. We're still in a desert right?

WATER. It's still a desert.

(*Enough chit-chat,* **WATER** *moves in.*)

WATER. I'm having trouble with something maybe you could help me out, Norte/Sur. I having trouble picturing you and my brother together. Hanging out and stuff.

NORTE/SUR. Yeah we used to play shoot 'em up bang bang...

(*This does not impress* **WATER.**)

NORTE/SUR. Let me say this about your brother. He's the
only *vato* that ever encouraged me to write, he got me
in a *chignon* screenwriting class at Universal Studios for
Latino writers taught by a real Jewish guy.

WATER. Really?

NORTE/SUR. Oh yeah, I even hung out with Brian Grazer and
Opie, yeah, I gave them their street cred and they got
me an expert adviser gig on a Tom Cruise gang movie.
I gotta go to Scientology once a week, but it ain't so bad.

WATER. I like the poem you read at my brother's funeral.

NORTE/SUR. Yeah?

WATER. It had an elliptical quality.

NORTE/SUR. I get that from my mother, she got seizures
real bad, rolling on the floor and what not.

WATER. That's not what I meant...

NORTE/SUR. I'm just bullshitting you man, I know what it
means. You think I write in circles.

WATER. Beautiful circles. Where's your sketch book now?

NORTE/SUR. My piece book? Never leaves my side.

WATER. Can I see it?

(**NORTE/SUR** *offers the book,* **WATER** *quickly finds his
brothers name.*)

WATER. My brother's name is all over this damn thing.

NORTE/SUR. Well yeah, he was my road dawg, aye.

(**NORTE/SUR** *points to a page.*)

NORTE/SUR. There goes the story of how I got my name.
See, a couple of months after I got out of the hospi-
tal, your brother took me up to Malibu Canyon, they
gotta sweatlodge up there you know, so I got to take
off all my clothes, my dockers, my black shirt that goes
real nice with my lucky lugz, so I'm naked right, and a
couple of the hippies *vatos* and this very large female,
help me into the lodge. Your brother stood just outside the lodge watching my stuff.

But inside, it was real hot in there I swear, I never felt
anything like it, my skin was burning but it felt real
good kinda, like all the bad things I had done were

burning off my skin you know?

I started crying in there bro, I couldn't stop, I felt sad for all the homies I lost, and all the ones I shot, thank goodness I was sweating cause nobody could see me crying you know. But the one old Indian *vato*, the elder he knew I was crying. He just leaned over and whispered in my ear that I now had a new name...

(**WATER** *reads from the book.*)

WATER. *Norte/Sur.*

NORTE/SUR. *Norte/Sur.* First thing that came to my mind was *hejole*, that name is gonna get me killed you know, but the Elder said no, that I was protected.

And you know something, when I crawled out of that lodge, I crawled like a baby, in the mud and dirt, I crawled out of there using my *brasos* like this you know, like a brown worm. I was being reborn or some shit like that you know, I lay there on my back, looking up at the Malibu sky, the stars up there you know, I ain't never seen them like that, all twinkling and shit.

(*This hits* **WATER**, **NORTE/SUR** *offers:*)

NORTE/SUR. *Maestro Jose* even allowed me the privilege of holding the Eagle Feather.

Do you wanna pray to the four directions with me Gilbert? We'll do it so that your *carnal* has a safe ride home to the Spirit World.

WATER. I don't think so. I'm going to have to ask you if I can hang on to your book.

NORTE/SUR. Why?

WATER. I have to protect my brother.

NORTE/SUR. And yourself, eh?

WATER. Nothing personal Norte/Sur, I don't know what else is in here. Could be full of all kinds of stuff.

NORTE/SUR. I don't lie *ese.* I mean used to lie plenty but not since I started going to *Kaballa.* My therapist thought it might be good for me.

(**WATER** *looks out for a long beat.* **WATER** *looks out over the audience.*)

WATER. Rose Hills. Feels lonely up here.

(*A beat goes bye.*)

NORTE/SUR. Go home senator, take a long shower, eat fresh field greens with organic balsamic vinegar and try to learn what the *Gringos* and Jews already know about power.

WATER. And what is that, oh great wise *cholo*?

NORTE/SUR. One - to have power and not use it. Two - if you do have it, spread it around. You Hispanics are still in your infancy with *pinche* power and it makes me sick. "I got it, so you can't have none."

WATER. Anything else?

NORTE/SUR. Yeah, learn the words to *De Colores* goddamm it.

WATER. I will take that under advisement.

NORTE/SUR. And learn to respect the Four Directions like the Indian Elder does. You might want to get all spiritual and shit like me. I'm enlightened like a motherfucker.

WATER. Is this where we pour the 40 ouncer's on my brother?

NORTE/SUR. Did The Mayor call you yet?

(**WATER** *shakes head no.*)

NORTE/SUR. He will. Underneath those expensive suits beats the heart of a homey who got kicked out of Cathedral High School.

WATER. All rivers reach the sea.

(**NORTE/SUR** *shakes his head no.*)

WATER. So, what are your plans Norte/Sur?

NORTE/SUR. I got an ol' lady now.

WATER. Is that so?

NORTE/SUR. She's in a chair too but we can still clack.

WATER. I'm happy for you.

NORTE/SUR. She was Miss Montebello 1989, aye.

WATER. Royalty eh?

NORTE/SUR. Oh yeah. She's still got some of the crown lodged in her brain but she ain't retarded or nothing. After I see her I gotta go back to the hood and make

things right with some little homey's I know. It's my
duty to tell them of the cautionary tale and destructive
nature of water and power.

Youngsters gotta learn, got to recognize, that the cold
heart of Hispanic ambition can leave your soul as dry
as the Owens Valley.

WATER. Do me a favor <u>Mr.</u> Norte/Sur, be sure to tell your
little homey's that being a *cholo* ain't all that. Don't get
all romantic about jumping them into the life – do not
have them *cholo* up. And you tell them that no good
ever <u>came</u> from a dead cop.

NORTE/SUR. Agreed. I'd like to show them that piece book
there.

WATER. Absolutely not.

NORTE/SUR. I would show them the pages of Gibby and
Gabby, and they would know that the twins were
blessed, that the bro's outsmarted the Lords of Death
but that there was a price to pay.

(**WATER** *leans down to the grave overcome.*)

There was a price to pay.

WATER. *(silent)* Yeah.

NORTE/SUR. You were your *carnal's* back up.

WATER. And for that I can feel proud?

NORTE/SUR. Where I come from back up is paramount.

WATER. Gangbanger philosophy.

NORTE/SUR. LA gangs will never die senator, ever. The City
of Angels needs her soldiers, she hungers for them.
Even if they're gangsters in suits and ties.

(**WATER** *can only look away.*)

NORTE/SUR. Are you mad at him?

WATER. *(so hard to answer that)* When did he decide to do it
Norte/Sur? At what moment?

NORTE/SUR. For my money, he did it the moment he figured out that all the bad things he did would go with
him. The fallout, the bad press. He set you up, bro.

You went up in the polls, got your Cesar Chavez River

Green Space *chingadera* passed, everybody still loves
The Twins homes. Even his fellow officers posted a nice
obituary on the bulletin board up at the firing range.
True Blue Vato.

A real marine. He kept his promise to you, to your
pops, to his city.

That's Power, that's your carnal right there, that's how
the Eastside rolls. And it's all carefully noted in those
pages. Nothing to fear in my piece book *ese*.

(**WATER** *offers – reaching over the grave – the Piece Book
back to* **NORTE/SUR**.)

NORTE/SUR. Nah, it belongs to you now. Learn more about
your bro aye. He's in there. All of him.

(**WATER** *holds the piece book with a certain affection.*
NORTE/SUR *offers:*)

NORTE/SUR. *(delicately)* I would have to say that some good
came from this dead cop.

WATER. Hey, why don't we do your little four directions
thing now.

NORTE/SUR. *Orale* Water, I'll do the In & Out fast food version.

(*We hear a flock of Canadian Geese fly over. As* **NORTE/
SUR** *reaches for his Eagle Feather:*)

NORTE/SUR. Nice ducks.

WATER. Canada Geese.

NORTE/SUR. Canadian Geese in the City of Industry?

WATER. Technically we're in Whittier.

NORTE/SUR. Even worser. Okay let's do this. First, we face
the North, no, lets do the South first.

(*The guys are clumsy in their initial effort as* **WATER**
goes to his knees.)

NORTE/SUR. You don't have to get on your knees aye.
Okay, toward our ancestors our brothers and sisters
from across the border, *el otro lado.*

Next we must face the, uh, West, yeah, where the sun
sets and we give thanks for the end of the day, that no
harm will come to any homey…

WATER. Or cop…

NORTE/SUR. *Simon.* To the North where we see a traffic jam on the Pomona freeway. In El Norte where Deer Dancer lives as well. And finally we turn to the East where Grandmother Moon's lives. She will see her sons shine again. We must humble ourselves to her. Ho.

WATER. Ho.

NORTE/SUR. That's it, that's all I know. He can rest now. Let him rest loco.

(**WATER** *agrees.* **NORTE/SUR** *puts away his feather.*)

WATER. Can I drop you off somewhere.

NORTE/SUR. Think I'll hang out here with your *carnal* just a taste longer.

WATER. Okay, well, uh, look, let me know if you need a letter of recommendation or anything like that.

NORTE/SUR. Let me know if *you* need one.

WATER. I gotta bail.

(**WATER** *heads off but is stopped in his tracks. He has found an amazing drawing of the twins.* **POWER,** *resplendent in his lovely uniform,* **POWER** *in his usual impeccable suit, both crouched down like the Homeboys do.*)

NORTE/SUR. The Twins *are* the eastside.

WATER. They were once.

NORTE/SUR. Nah, Water and Power forever, homes.

(**WATER** *turns to* **NORTE/SUR** *holding the open book over his heart show.*)

NORTE/SUR. *Con safos.*

WATER. *Con safos.* Thank you bro.

(**NORTE/SUR** *nods. The men touch their hearts and* **WATER** *is gone.*)

(**NORTE/SUR** *is center stage, he motions for somebody to join him. Enter the young* **DEER DANCER** *homeboy. This time the* **DEER DANCER** *wears the antlers, black bandana, black Pendleton, baggie kakis and shiny black shoes.*)

(NORTE/SUR motions for the boy to stand directly in front of him.)

(NORTE/SUR motions for the boy to remove: antlers, black shirt, bandana and the black shoes.)

(The black shoes go into NORTE/SUR's side bag. The rest of the garb is placed gently on the grave of Power.)

(NORTE/SUR is ending a few cycles here.)

(The gangbanging and ambitious Hispanic cycle both come to a momentary end with this NORTE/SUR action – we must know this as an audience.)

(The boy has a little boy shirt on and is now barefoot.)

(He looks like what he is, just a boy.)

(The BOY moves a few reluctant feet away from NORTE/SUR.)

(NORTE/SUR produces a baseball.)

(NORTE/SUR tosses the ball to the DEER DANCER.)

(A beat, the BOY looks back, unsure.)

NORTE/SUR. Go on. Play. Be a kid. Go...

(The BOY tears off through the house vaum like any kid would.)

(We hear the child squeal with delight and a child's laugh.)

(NORTE/SUR watches the kid scram, as satisfying smile begins to crosses his face.)

(The Rain Song reprises.)

(NORTE/SUR does a lovely little twirl with the wheelchair.)

(His dance: his gentle closing of this ceremonial circle.)

(Lights slowly fade.)

(END OF PLAY)

From the Reviews of
WATER & POWER...

"Fans of Culture Clash's chicano-inflected, spoken-word-erupting performance art needn't worry that they've lost sight of their signature gifts. Montoya's latest piece, a tale of brothers and a morass of local and national corruption, daringly bundles these elements into tragedy...A significant step in an ambitious new direction."
- *Los Angeles Times*

"*Water & Power* possesses some of the familiar untamed wildness and a good deal of the old Clash comedy. But Montoya's writing here has psychological weight, too. He manages to compress the events of one violent night and its aftermath into an episodic play riddled with a specifically Latin fatalism."
- Anne Marie Welsh, *San Diego Critic*

"A bold announcement of Culture Clash's passage into new theatrical realms...Montoya's muscular writing is a worthy match for the ruthless power politics the play depicts...The play has its own power to shake up theatergoers."
- *The San Diego Union-Tribune*

"Original and exciting...Darkly funny and vividly realized...
CRITICS PICK"
- *The San Diego Union-Tribune*

"Exciting, chilling, often hilarious - both the writing and the performance are unbuttoned and ebullient."
- *North County Times*

"Colorful and imaginative...will surely touch your heart."
- *San Diego CityBeat*

"A tale for our time...highly dramatic, throughly intriguing and thought provoking...with a touch of magic and the poetry of the street and the heart. You'll be thinking about the play long after its over. A wonderful piece of work."
- Pat Launer, KSDS Radio